AF445307

# Curse of the Black Horn

by

Kemal Onor

Copyright Kemal Onor 2024

ALL RIGHTS RESERVED

With loving dedication to the few

who never doubted

and never left

1

The roads had been bumpy for some time. The brown minivan rocked and jumped, kicking stones into the undercarriage of the vehicle that had cost them six hundred dollars cash. Roger glanced down at the fuel gauge. The thing didn't work. James and Carter sat in the back seat. He slowed the car down and moved to the edge of the road.

"Could you check the math?" said Roger as though speaking to no one in particular. Roger's wife, Danielle, sat in the front passenger seat. Without a word, she glanced at a legal pad and read down the list of figures. Since running out of fuel in upstate New York, they had been ticking off mile markers. It was summer, and already, the minivan felt like a volcano. The windows and ragged interior held heat like an iron rod. Even the windows, which could only be pushed out, seemed to reflect more sunlight in on them. Nothing but hot, sticky air came in. They were being cooked in that oven of a car. With the intense heat, Carter and James had surrendered their shirts. They both sat in bathing suits as though they were on their way to spend a day at a pool or a lake. Despite the heat, Carter wore a thick beanie over his head. Roger glanced in the review mirror and saw that the hat still had the bulge in the center of his son's forehead. James wore a better-suited baseball cap that he had turned backwards. James insisted on being like his older brother.

"We should have another fifty miles," said Danielle. Roger turned his eyes back to the road and moved the car slowly along.

"Look, dad, cows," said Carter. Along the edge of the road was a fence, and several cows stood about eating grass. Roger leaned out his window as he drove.

"Can we stop? Please," said James and Carter. Roger did not respond. He slowed the car, but his eyes were already scanning the field.

"A short break wouldn't be so bad, dear," said Danielle.

"We really shouldn't," said Roger. He steadily increased the speed and drove past the field. James and Carter sat back down in their seats. Roger narrowed his eyes as the speed of the minivan kicked up dirt and dust behind them. The road continued to jostle the vehicle like they were in the middle of an earthquake. Roger looked back to the review mirror. A twinge of anger struck him. His nostrils flared. Carter had removed his beanie. His hair was matted to his forehead with a layer of sweat. And there, poking through like a shorn stump. A fracture of bone that broke through a dirty ground was the strange growth. It jutted out like a nub of smooth, weathered stone. Carter scratched at the hard carapace that spread around the split skin to let the strange growth sprout.

"Carter," said Roger. He made eye contact with his son in the mirror.

"Dad, it itches," said Carter.

"I know, but you have to keep your hat on." It was the best solution they could devise for transporting their son. For a while, it had been a bump on Carter's head as though the thing was pushing out from his son's brain like a tumor. But now it was like a horn that had wormed through the skull, seeking the surface. An extension of thought driven out of his son's crammed mind. It stuck out straight as a thorn.

Roger's gaze fell and lingered on the exposed bone. The thing was growing. He worried how much longer it would get. Would it just keep on growing until it was a rhino horn extending into the ceiling of the minivan? Roger knew the exact moment when the thing had sprouted. He thought back to the night, right before Carter came into their room on silent feet. It was more than just a nightmare.

He had said he had a headache. They had checked him for a fever, feeling his son's forehead. At the time, they thought he had only accidentally bumped his head on something. The next morning, though, the skin broke. There was a small protrusion of a bloody splinter through skin. The thing had been small once. Now, like so many things, it was growing. When would it stop? Did it have a capacity to reach? Was it like a stalk of grass, a tree? Was it like something in the wild that would keep growing unless cut or removed? Roger was soon lost in thought. They were heading north. Being as secretive about the whole matter as they could be. There were always too many eyes watching. Too many chance glances, even on the highway. If a trucker were to look down or another curious child to glance out his window, the secret would be out.

Mom, look, that boy has a horn sticking out of his head. The thought of discovery clenched Roger's gut. His insides were already hardened. He did the best he could to concentrate on the road ahead of them.

"Carter, put the hat on now," said Roger. The terrible horn sickened him. The worst part was when the horn broke through the skin, the soft flesh around it turned red, irritated, and bloody. Carter had screamed and howled as they tried to clean it. They had tried originally to remove it themselves. Pulling and even taking a pair of kitchen shears to it. The strange growth was deeply rooted, attached to their son's brain. Carter had screamed like his parents were trying to murder him. Now, they were seeking a specialist. Someone who could remove the growth, sew the split skin, and return their son to normal. They knew it would not do to bring him to the emergency room. There was no description they could find on the internet for why a sudden horn was growing out of their son's forehead. They had managed to find a remote doctor who could do the job in secrecy. So far, it was their best option. Roger's eyes flickered between the road and the reflection of his son in the rearview mirror. He hadn't been sleeping well since they had started driving. His head felt like it was filling with stones.

"Alright. You guys know the rules!" said Roger, trying to make it sound as much like a game as possible. He still couldn't shake the taste that was left in his mouth. It wasn't his fault. It couldn't be. The minivan idled, and he checked one last time to make sure both Carter and James were lying face down in the back. He urged the car onto a paved road when he couldn't see their heads. They would be stopping in town for gas and a cup of coffee. Danielle tossed a blanket over the back seats, and just like that, the children were stolen goods being covered and hidden.

Now, all Roger had to do was calm his mind. He listened to his breathing, the rhythm it made. But that reminded him of the noises they had made the night before everything started. The primal sounds as they threw their bodies together like magnesium rods against metal, driving against each other, desperate to create a spark. He turned the radio on. The station was a northern country station that was only partially conceived. The twangy notes were washed in a buzz of static. For the moment, it was better than enduring the silence. He desperately needed something for his mind to latch onto.

Something to get him away from the guilt that felt tattooed across his belly fat.

All Danielle needed to do was lift his shirt, and there it would be – plainly written – in black ink across his pale mid-section. Like a criminal branded with his prison number. But she hadn't noticed. Maybe he was too good at his deceitful ways, or perhaps she knew and didn't care to expose him for what he was. There would be no splitting up, not until they had solved the problem of their son's strange growth. Now and then, he caught the hot, dry voices of Carter and James. He knew their mouths would be filled with the heated dust of the floor. Like puffs of air, or fragrant scents, caught now and then on a breeze, their voices rose from the backseats.

"I need a coffee," said Roger. He parked the car on the side of the road and stared at the distance to the coffee shop. No one was walking along the sidewalk, but Roger was still reluctant to leave his family. Maybe his need for sleep was starting to get to him. "Will you keep the car going? I'll be right back." Again, he didn't turn to look at Danielle. He hadn't looked her in the face since they had left.

"Go get a coffee. We'll be alright," said Danielle. He could feel her look like a hand resting against the side of his face. Like her gaze still held the affection for him that it had when they first met in college.

"Okay." He moved over in his seat and sensed his wife move over too, ready to make the switch, like one of them was a drunk teenager. And one had sobered up a half hour ago. He opened his door and jumped out into the road. He closed the door and caught his wife now in the driver's seat. She slowly pulled away, and he turned to get on the sidewalk and make his way to the coffee shop.

It was the first time they had been separated since leaving home. His skin felt grimy, like it was covered in dust and salt. He wore the miles from Erie, Pennsylvania, like a winter coat. The sun overhead was intense, but the air felt cool on his skin after spending the last five days in the minivan. His arms were frozen at his side like they were still gripping a steering wheel. He wiped his face and groaned. He desperately needed a cup of coffee. He slumped down the sidewalk, pressing the heels of his hands against his sunken eyes. The coffee shop was relatively empty. By Roger's guess, it was late afternoon, so it was the time before an afternoon cup of coffee for the teachers and office workers on their way home. A young group of college-age kids sat in a corner with a laptop on the table. They were all dressed identically with cheap clothes that were much too small for their long, athletic frames.

Roger glanced about the small shop without making eye contact with anyone. He made his way to the restroom. The ugly fluorescent light revealed his skin to look like it was melting off his skeleton. His eyes were marked by deep bruises. He blinked at his reflection, feeling a sickness in his gut. There was still a light, near indiscernible mark on his collar. It could have just as easily been a fleck of dried blood, but he knew what it really was: women's lipstick. He grabbed a paper towel and wadded it, putting it under a stream of water.

He paused. The image of the woman with the color dragged across her lips came to his mind. She had been so lovely. Her hair curled and cropped at her shoulders. He closed his eyes, breathed in deeply through his nose, and saw her face. His nostrils flared as they did when she stood so near him. The allure of her perfume coiling around him, like vines wrapping around his legs, binding the two together. He wiped at the stain on his collar, and a dark, wet mark replaced the color. He tried dabbing at it, letting the stain lift little by little. It was hardly noticeable before, but now it stood out against the light shade of his shirt.

He attempted to dry the spot with several paper towels. t could just as easily have been a puddle of sweat. They had all been sweating in that hot box of a car. That would be his excuse f Danielle asked about it. But so far, she had not even asked about the rouge stain on his neck.

Roger realized she was probably out there circling, waiting for him to get coffee. He collected himself and left the restroom. The café had not changed. No one new had come along, and if they had, they simply grabbed their cup and left. Roger looked down at his shoes as he approached the counter.

"Can I have a cup of coffee?" said Roger.

"For here or to go?" asked the employee.

"To go," said Roger, a bit short.

Only after the coffee was placed on the counter, and Roger paid did he pick his head up from his shoes. He decided to stand by the road where he had switched places with his wife in the driver's seat. He sipped his coffee. It was old but hot, and he felt his body receive the caffeine. The tension in his shoulders gave slightly like ice that is starting to soften, relinquishing its hold on a gutter drain, returning to water.

He hoped the thing protruding from Carter's forehead could be so easily removed. He hoped this doctor would be able to help. Maybe the thing didn't grow downward. Maybe it didn't have strong roots. He stood by the road, now and then taking a sip from his cup. Any moment, he expected the brown minivan would pull up alongside, and they would complete the transfer again. Roger dug his toes into the ground.

Time went by, and Roger caught the faces of drivers passing by. Each time someone looked over and saw him, he felt a sickening accusation. Like he was being accused of a terrible crime that he could not hope to defend himself against. All paths seemed to lead to the same bleak end. The electric chair. He finished his cup of coffee, but Danielle still had not arrived. Maybe she had decided to go ahead and get gas. They only had fifty miles left, and getting the car filled sooner rather than later would allow them to get out of town quicker. Roger already trembled with his nerves, feeling like they had been supercharged. All these people. He knew none of them knew him, and he knew none cared, that he was standing outside a coffee shop drinking a cup of coffee. There was nothing suspicious about it. Everyone was so preoccupied with their own lives; they would all forget about the man standing outside, waiting for his wife to pick him up, by the time they reached the first stop sign. They would already be thinking of how to put the kids to bed that night and about work or grabbing a beer.

He closed his eyes and tried to conjure the woman's face. She had been studying Latin, which had been why her home smelled like Italian cooking and Middle Eastern spices. The yellow dust like so much crushed flower petals. Like so much sun-soaked paper and sand swept through the ages to waft in the kitchen air, circling above your head and dancing through the senses like a memory. The wine had been exquisitely sharp. Maybe that was the taste he could not shake from his mouth. It lay there like a beetle latched into the center of his tongue.

Roger sat down on the sidewalk. There was still no sign of Danielle and the brown minivan. He reached into his pocket and took out his phone. He pulled up Danielle's number, pushed call, and put the phone to his ear. He listened to the ring. There was no answer. Roger left a brief message. Few words were all the two of them were able to manage for one another. He sat there sweating in the afternoon sun. He played over the map in his head. They went from Erie, Pennsylvania, and avoided any major city through upstate New York. Taking poor roads had added to the time the trip was taking. So much time in the car. Now reaching the more rural states of the jumbled North East. When no one knew how much land there was to the west. Worry was starting to stir in Roger like the first winds of a maelstrom. He grimaced and folded in on himself. Where was Danielle? Why did she not answer her phone?

To hell with it, he thought. If he was going to have to wait for the minivan to come back around, the least he could do would be to get another cup of coffee and maybe try and wash off some of the miles in the bathroom sink. He stood, turning from the road, and went back to the coffee shop. Nothing had changed from his last visit. He scowled as he looked around again. The college students were still sitting there, gathered around the laptop on the table. Roger went straight to the restroom. He switched the faucet as hot as it would go, and let the water run until the lower part of the mirror started to fog. He cupped his hands under the burning stream and then splashed his face.

It stung, but he sighed and rubbed his face. The skin felt loose. He had lost weight. He took a wadded amount of paper towels and scrubbed his face and arms. He scrubbed himself until all his exposed skin glowed a bright, raw red. He stretched and smiled at his reflection. Water streamed from his hair. He looked like crap, but it was the most amazing shower he could ever remember taking in his life.

When he was done with his sink shower, he checked his phone. There was still no message. No missed call, not even so much as a text message. When he told her to keep the car running, he assumed she would circle until he came back. He had not planned on being gone so long. He grit his teeth and left the restroom. He left the coffee shop without getting a second cup. He could sense his anger rising. The outside air felt cool on his raw skin. He laughed at the thought that he had shed his traveling skin and revealed the true devil within. He didn't mind the irritation. He marched stiffly back to the spot where his wife had taken the car.

He thought of the vile possibility. Had she just been playing games with him? Had she been leading with him on? Toying with him until she had a chance to take the wheel? All at once, he felt incredibly foolish. He felt deceived. He made fists, and, sitting down, ground his knuckles against the sidewalk until they bled. Roger felt something in him awaken, like an ancient body rising from a grave. Maggoty arms shedding worms and dropping spiders and vile insects from their feeding. His corpse was reanimated. The sunlight seemed to crawl over his skin, slicing its teeth like tiny shards of broken glass all along his body. Digging in with the pressure of butterfly teeth. The thing in him was vengeful. It was maddened. It felt like living stone brimming with fire, hatred, and rage. He put the full force of his body against his knuckles. He pressed as hard as he could and scraped any amount of skin until he felt he was surely grinding bone against cement. He stood. A bead of blood ran down each finger, on each hand. That was when he saw the brown minivan making its way along the road.

2

Roger could only imagine how crazy he must have looked standing by the side of the road. Hair still wet and matted to his forehead. His skin raw, like he had been cooked. And his hands dripping blood onto the pavement. There was not enough to slick the ground, but there was enough that he could hear the wet slap as each bead struck the hot ground. So she had come back for him? She must have realized she could not do it alone. She must have gone all the way to the Canadian border before realizing she would need his help. Before accepting that they would not be able to abandon one another.

Roger looked down at his knuckles. The skin was scraped like he had dug his nails into the soft flesh. Like he had when he was a child. It had been Roger's nervous tick. Whenever his mother and father fought, Roger would sit down and scratch at the backs of his hands. If the arguments went on long enough, as they often did, it would not be uncommon for Roger to be wadding clumps of skin under his nails. That was why his mother always trimmed his nails as close to the cuticle as possible.

He was reminded of when his mother clipped his ring finger nail off. Blood had pooled there, and it took several days before he started to see a new nail grow back. The tip had been a snail without a shell, soft, pale pink. He looked up from his thoughts. Danielle idled the car, still sitting in the driver's seat, waiting for him to get in. He wiped his knuckles on his jeans, opened the door, and climbed into the passenger seat.

"I got gas," said Danielle. She motioned to the legal pad that was in the footwell. Roger bent down and picked up the legal pad. He saw the mark she made that meant they had filled the minivan. James and Carter were still on the floor. The blanket had been tossed aside, but the two boys lay asleep on the floor. Danielle had done what she could to keep Carter's growing horn covered by the blanket. Roger knew she hated the strange growth as much, if not more, than he did.

Roger flexed his hands, and a line of blood oozed out the tops of his knuckles like each was an individual crying fountain.

"What happened to your hand?" asked Danielle. Roger glanced away.

"I fell," said Roger. "How long have they been asleep for?"

"About a half hour."

"Would you like me to drive?"

"No, it's fine." She paused, mouth parted, jaw hanging loose.

"I hate this" she said with a weak smile.

They both glanced to the rearview mirror and looked at their sons sprawled as comfortably as they could get in the back seats. Roger felt the twist of guilt. The way James and Carter slept so peacefully. He wished he could achieve such innocence. The demons would never allow it, though. He was a felon. Anytime he closed his eyes, he would hear the shrill voices of the accusers: Guilty! Guilty! They shrieked in high-octave voices. Raking his mind like so much gravel over dirt.

"Another hour or so," said Roger. He lounged back in his seat. "Now I need some sleep." Roger shut his eyes and leaned the seat back. Snippets of memory played in his mind. The woman, with her strange oddities. He thought of all the clutter in her small apartment. The cardboard boxes lining one wall like she was planning a move. He couldn't remember the reason she gave for why the boxes were so numerous. Maybe she simply never unpacked her things. No, that wasn't it. He thought about it, letting the minivan's oppressive heat blanket him like a lover's body. Roger soon found himself in a state of lucid dreams. He was drifting between thought and slumber. His mind felt as if it were a sail mast with the wind constantly shifting; never holding one direction for too long, rocking back and forth, teetering, with micro-adjustments.

Everything about that night felt like it had been crumpled up and thrown into a waste bin. Some things were salvageable, but others were more distorted and damaged. It would take a good deal of time for him to piece his thoughts together. Fortunately, he had a lot of time to think. Roger let his chin drop to the side, and he slept.

About a half hour later, he felt Danielle's fingers jabbing into his ribs. He apprehensively opened his eyes and put his dirty knuckles against his eye sockets.

"Roger, wake up," said Danielle. There was an edge to her voice, and Roger's mind flicked on all at once. Even though he had slept for almost a half hour, he did not feel rested. If anything, he felt even more tired now than when he shut his eyes. But the edge in Danielle's voice jabbed at him with blaring alarm. He sat up, blinking, trying to shake the fatigue of his napping. The sun was still bright, and the van was still desert hot. He tried to look around for what might cause the edge in Danielle's voice. Had she put the pieces together? What if she had lifted his shirt and caught the message on his pale skin?

"Wake up, what should we do?" said Danielle. She was pointing now, and Roger followed her extended hand to the road ahead. Traffic was at a standstill. Two police vehicles were parked on either side of the road. Three officers were standing and leaning in on people's windows. Roger realized why Danielle had woken him. He realized why she had the edge to her voice.

"We'll be fine," he said. "We haven't done anything wrong, after all. It's probably just a checkpoint. Holiday weekend, maybe?"

"What if they want to search the car?"

"They won't," he said with surprising calmness.

Slowly, traffic moved, like links being pulled through a gear change. The line of cars stuttered and stopped as each car approached the checkpoint. Roger heard Danielle's breathing draw and pull like a tide raking over land.

"It's okay," he said. He reached over and took his wife's hand. He felt the tremor in her body, the tightened squeeze like she was bracing for something terrible to jump from the darkness. Something beyond horrible. Not a fictional monster with large menacing teeth, but a police officer with a quick trigger finger and an all-too-quick judgment about mental state. Her father had been shot right in his own driveway.

She shook in her seat. Body tensed, muscles straining. Her gaze cold. It was hurt, and it was an iron resolve.

"It's okay," said Roger, speaking low and soft. He knew it would not do any of them any good for Danielle to go off into her tirade about police brutality. She brought the minivan to a stop. She simply sat in the driver's seat for a moment, unwilling so long that even whispers sounded like they were filled with so much desert sand. Like the weight of everything had doubled, tripled. They were all sweating once more.

"Do you want to stop? Check it out," said Danielle. Even though she had regained her composure, her face still held the tear marks, and there were spots on her face where the skin had been rubbed harder than others, causing red spots of irritation. She was like a riverbed with furrows drawn across the bottom. Roger did not respond. He watched Carter worm a finger up the front of his scalp.

"Does it hurt, Carter? said Roger. Carter looked up.

"It just itches," said Carter.

Five miles later, on a long, uninhabited road, they pulled the car over. Roger got out of his seat and went into the back of the minivan. He carefully started to lift the beanie from Carter's head. The hat started to smell, absorbing so much of Carter's sweat and blood. As Roger pulled the beanie off, he found the hat reluctant to be removed. The fabric felt fused to Carter's forehead. Carter made a sound as the hat was taken off. The terrible horn came into view. The tip of the horn was not a smooth dome. Nor did it have a clear tip, like a rhino horn or an elephant's tusk. The way the thing grew, the tip resembled a shard of broken shale stone. Roger wondered if the horn would grow layers like rings on a tree. It was a clean bone white. Roger saw that Carter's picking at the hard skin had caused the young boy's forehead to ooze blood. It had then dried and glued the hat to his son's forehead.

"How does it look?" asked Danielle. She had watched her husband crouched in the back seat, looking inches away from the terrible horn. The idea that her oldest son was growing a horn out of his head. It sent a shiver through her. She shuttered at the thought of blood.

"Can you hand me the first-aid kit?" said Roger.

"What about me?" asked James. "Look at my forehead next, Dad." He removed his backward baseball cap. He swept his bangs back and exposed his clean, unbroken forehead.

"James, come up front with mommy," said Danielle. She had the first-aid kit in hand. James moved towards the front and, after passing the first-aid kit to his father, sat down in the front, where Danielle started to pinch and examine James's forehead. Roger took the kit. Opening it like a surgeon opening his bag of tools for cutting, scraping, and examining.

Roger set the kit in the seat beside Carter; he took a cotton ball and put some antibacterial on it.

"It's okay, relax." Carter made a face and looked away from his father. The horn followed the turn of his head. Roger had been the one to take the kitchen shears to the horn. A memory of pain that Roger knew still lived in Carter. Roger coaxed his son to look back.

He touched the spot of dried blood around the horn with the cotton swab. There was an immediate reaction. Carter jumped back like Roger touched his son with a glowing ember. Carter started screaming, the high-pitched child scream of murder.

"Don't touch it!" screamed Carter. He started scrambling away from his father. Climbing over seats, making his body as small as he could. Carter was a mouse in a burning building, frantically seeking an exit.

"Carter," said Roger, calm and soft.

"It hurts when you touch it!" cried Carter. He was in the back of the minivan, kicking the back door as hard as he could, trying to escape, trying to get away. James started screaming, too, but his screaming was more children's fun and games. Carter was screaming bloody murder. He rolled around in the back hatch. He pounded everything he could get his fists or feet to touch. Danielle took James in her lap. Carter pleaded and rolled around, wailing like a banshee. Then he started to throw himself at the window. He attacked it with his head lowered.

"Carter! Carter, stop!" The words stuck in Roger and Danielle's throats. Roger was now reaching over the backseats.

"Don't!" Screamed Carter. He yelled his command like a bell striking midnight on a bleak winter night. Ghosts drifting over snow. Shadows melting in moonlight. Horrible eyes, faces, and mouths, watching you from frosted tree branches. Winking like starlight in an inky sky.

There was the sound of glass being scraped. Then, a hairline fracture. Carter threw himself like an enraged ram at the back window. He was small enough that he only had to slightly bend at the spine to let himself stand so he could force himself on the window. The glass spiderwebbed. Roger grabbed his son and pulled him, screaming and squirming away from the broken window. Glass shot out in a spray of electricity and light.

Where the horn had punctured the glass was a gaping hole the size of a golf ball.

"Carter, Carter, calm down. I'm not going to touch it," said Roger. Carter heaved. His lower lip quivered like he was mumbling to himself. Carter breathed through his teeth and sniffed. For the moment, the storm had passed. He was bleeding, a slash above his eyebrows where his brow had struck the glass. It was a ragged cut with tiny shards of glass embedded like frost on a window.

"Can I fix you up?" said Roger, trying to remain calm. Carter nodded. Roger took a pair of tweezers from the kit and went to work pulling the shards of glass trapped in the soft skin outside the hardened, red carapace that formed around the horn like a moat of red earth.

"Maybe we need a break from traveling?" said Danielle. James shuffled from his mother's lap and scampered back to Roger and Carter.

"Dad, can I have a band-aid?" said James. Roger had pulled out as much of the glass as he could, and was tentatively cleaning the blood. He was careful not to go too close to the horn. Even though flecks of blood were on the white bone, Roger knew it would be better to leave it alone. He made a face, trying to size up the exposed bone. Maybe the horn was working its way out of his son's head. What if it was like a splinter that the body was working to remove? Again, Roger wondered and questioned how big the thing would grow. He put a bandage on James's forehead.

"I think that's a good idea," said Roger. "But let's put some more miles in first." He left his sons in the back of the minivan and returned to the front of the car. Danielle started the engine up, and they pulled back onto the road.

"You look so tired," said Danielle. She managed a weak smile. "I think we should spend a night –

"I don't think we can risk it. What if someone sees him?" said Roger.

"He can stay in the room, and we'll make sure he keeps his hat on." She made a small circle on her cheek as though scrubbing a patch of dirt. "One night, a hot shower, then we'll be on our way." Roger was looking straight ahead, staring down the road. It had been a while since they had passed anyone on the road. James and Carter had settled into the back seat. Roger glanced in the rearview.

They were both squirming in the backseat, stretching their legs, trying to make as much room for their small bodies to relax. It had been a long time since they had been able to take a breath. Roger was quiet as he watched the worming, antsy bodies of his children in the back seat.

"Do you have a place in mind?"

"There might be a small place in about twenty minutes."

Roger nodded. Danielle was right about the time of around twenty minutes. However, it was closer to a half hour when the trees and low swamps that lined the road on both sides gave way to more developed areas. They were on the outskirts of a small town. Green tree-filled mountains rose around the small town, and a river ran along the side of the road. Roger checked to make sure Carter was wearing his hat. He was, but Roger felt his stomach twisting like worms in the ground, blindly mouthing their way in the dirt.

They passed a graveyard to the left and entered the small town proper.

"Is this the place?" asked Roger. Danielle was looking around the empty roads. Roger knew she was thinking about memories from years ago like she was studying a photo album of black and white pictures aged and stained by time.

"Let's see," said Danielle. She clicked her tongue and pulled out her phone. "It should still be here." Danielle drove slowly through the hamlet.  They found The Old Motor Inn Motel. A horseshoe shaped motel at the top of a short hill. The place looked relatively remote from any real action of a main drag. It made Roger feel a little easier about the idea of spending a night in an actual bed. It had been over a week since he and Danielle slept in the same bed. Over a week since their lives had been rattled by the discovery of the horn growing out of their son's head. Over a week since he had met the strange woman and drank her wine.

The parking lot was empty for the most part, with only a couple of vehicles covered with dirt and mud occupying a corner of the lot. Probably reserved for staff, thought Roger. Even with his caution, Roger started to warm up to the idea. They all could really use a shower and a chance for a good night's sleep in a proper bed. His neck had been tightening over the past days of sleeping in a car.

Danielle pulled into the parking lot and turned the car off. She checked the odometer and noted on the legal pad how long they had traveled since filling the vehicle up.

"Alright, boys," said Danielle. "I want your best behavior. No roughhousing until we're in the room, understand?"

"We're not sleeping in the car?" said James. During the first few nights of sleeping in the car, James was excited. But after a while, when Carter complained about wanting to sleep in his real bed, the novelty of sleeping on the road wore off.

"Let's go!" said Carter.

"Do you understand?" said Danielle.

"Yes!" said James and Carter. Roger was studying the parking lot and trying to see if he could make out the check-in office.

"Okay," said Roger. "We're here one night." Both Roger and Danielle let out a sigh before opening their door. Roger made his way for the office, and Danielle was left to care for James and Carter. Roger found an old man sitting behind a computer.

"Hello, we'd like to rent a room," said Roger.

"Let's set you folks up. I have a room with two beds available," said the front desk man.

"We'll take it," said Roger. "How much is it?" Roger was eager to get out of the small office. Something about the design of the old place made him feel like he had stepped backward in time. The ceiling was low. It looked like the place had not been updated since it was first built.

"Your name?" The old man looked at him through thick glasses.

"Rog –"

He stopped. Realizing that this was the first interaction with someone since they had set out to find the doctor who would remove the horn. He did not say anything for a second. They had wanted to keep everything secret. Even though he could see no harm in giving his real name to this old bookkeeper, he felt it would be better to keep everything hidden.

"Ronald," said Roger. It was the name he gave when he went to the bars alone. Of course, it was close enough to his real name that he didn't need to pretend too hard or work to remember to respond to his new name. But it allowed him to feel a little better about his escapades. Now and then, he would mix it up if he could. He would plan a name before going out. Sometimes, he would go by Jack. Sometimes, he would go by Stephen. At the moment, with the man looking at him, he was unprepared.

The feeling reminded him of when he had come across the woman; before everything began. Before his son came into their room and complained about a headache. Before he felt his son's head and touched the horn for the first time, when he felt it pushing against the skin, like a snapped femur. Roger gapped at the man. Already, he regretted the decision to take a break from traveling.

"Do you have a bathroom?" asked Roger.

"We do." The desk clerk handed Roger a pair of keys and pointed toward the bathroom. Roger took them and went to the bathroom. He was shaking. For the life of him, he could not remember what name he had given the woman. He looked at his reflection in the mirror. He felt disgusted. He grabbed the bathroom sink, leaning forward as though he might throw up. Something in him was wrong. He spit into the sink, arms shaking. The room felt like it was spinning. Every time he thought of that night, it made him ill.

Roger looked at his tired, worn reflection in the bathroom mirror. All he needed was a good night's rest and a hot shower. He jangled the keys, sticking them in his pocket, and went to find Danielle and the boys. When he found them, they made their way to the room number on the set of keys. Their room was number sixteen. James and Carter were talking loudly to one another. Roger opened the door, and they entered their room.

"Let's turn on some AC," said Danielle. "That van is so hot, I feel like I've melted." She went to the AC unit and turned it on high. A cold blast of air soon permeated the room. There were two beds in the small motel room. The boys started jumping on one bed, and Roger, still feeling nauseous, fell onto his back on the other. He blinked and stared at the ceiling.

"I'm taking a shower," said Danielle. Roger felt his body sinking into the bed. His muscles relaxed, and his skin felt coated in liquid metal. The chill of the AC unit made the hair on his arms stand up, but it was a lot better than sweating in that minivan. The boys were laughing and jumping up and down on the bed. Roger was too tired to care much. His mind buzzed like an overheated engine that had been smoking for some time and revving without oil. The gears grinding and slipping. Now, his mind had a moment to stop. He sensed himself reeling. The room felt like it was spinning, just like he had felt in the bathroom. Maybe it wasn't just the room spinning, but the world. Roger shut his eyes and tried to stop the feeling that he was being pulled down a drain pipe. He felt himself spinning, circling. He was dropping like an airplane that had lost an engine. Each time, Carter or James shot up from the bed; each time the springs sank under their weight, Roger felt himself pressed deeper against the bed. He was being flattened.

Then she was there. Standing in the middle of the motel room. His wife in the shower, and this woman. The one he kept secret. The one he would never let anyone know he knew. What was she doing here? How had she found him? She smiled at him without saying a word. Roger was in that lucid dream state where everything feels like you're looking at it from underwater, with sunlight filtering over the tops of waves. Everything is glowing and warm. What was her name again? He could not hope to remember. They had only met that one time. There could have been more meetings, but the matter started with Carter growing a horn.

As Roger floated in his thoughts, he wondered if the woman, Lucile, Wendy, or Janice, whatever it was. Had she done something to him? He could not grasp any of his ideas. It was like trying to grab clouds on a lake's surface. They were gone the moment he tried to reach for them. His mind empty, like so much air had been sucked out. He kept his eyes closed and listened to the sounds of his sons jumping on the bed beside him laughing and being able to still be children, despite the horn growing out of Carter's forehead.

He imagined Carter without the terrible horn, and he imagined both of them being like normal boys. He thought of them all as a normal family on a normal vacation. He could hear the sound of water running in the bathroom. He knew Danielle would likely turn the water as hot as she could. He soon fell back asleep.

When he woke, Danielle had her hair wrapped in a towel. She had a vibrant hue to her. Roger guessed she had scrubbed a lot of grim from the last days of travel. The boys were watching a TV show. They had stopped jumping and settled to sit on the end of the other bed.

Roger blinked and looked at the ceiling. He looked at the evening light that hung in the windows. The blood-red glare of a fiery sunset. Despite his sleep, Roger did not feel rested. His mind felt like it had been in a dryer set to tumble. It rolled around like a marble in a glass jar, racing wildly around in circles, generating noise as it went screaming around and around.

And he had dreamed of her. He could feel himself growing more suspicious of this woman. Unfortunately, that night felt bookended by mystery. He could not even rightly remember her name. His memory could only suggest words to him, but even if he managed to stumble upon it, he knew he could never be confident with her true name. Maybe it was better that he didn't know. It allowed him not to play dumb, but rather, he didn't know simply because he was dumb. Lucile or Linda felt closest, but he knew it could really be anything. He regretted the secrets he kept from Danielle.

"Do you want to shower?" said Danielle. She was flipping through a magazine and looking up now and then to see the boys enjoying their show.

"Is there hot water?" Roger asked. She smiled at him, innocent as a fawn. He felt that smile all the way in his stomach. He felt it shriek inside him, a blood-curdling scream that felt like it had claws. He felt his insides being brushed by long-nailed hands. He felt the hooked fingers digging into him, drawing blood like teeth into a chunk of meat. Slowly, Roger stood. He pressed his hands into his face, touching the dark bruise-like spots under his eyes. He breathed out and looked at his feet as he went to the shower. A heat still hung in the air of the small shower room. There was only a few degrees of difference; like passing a spot where somebody had stood on a street corner in August smoking. It was like a windswept perfume lingered in the shower room. The kind that roils with the hints of decay and autumn. The smell of time, of things decomposing. It had a touch of ancient times, of long-extinct civilizations. He could taste it on his tongue like a leaf of salted tobacco. It tasted foreign and yet familiar. His reflection still showed him as haggard. He could barely lift his head high enough to look himself in the eye. His head hung suspended.

Roger undressed and turned the shower on as hot as it would go. He let the room fill with steam. He got in the shower, and the water burned, but the feeling was heavenly. He stood in the shower, just letting the water roll down his back. He let the steam take him in its arms. The warmth of July took him and wrapped him like a caterpillar ready to turn into a chrysalis.

He was ready to burn his skin away. Shed the old layers. He wanted to remove the dirt, sweat, and grim from the days of travel. He wanted to be nothing more than bones and muscles.

When Roger left the shower room, evening had come to the windows of the motel. He felt clean and was feeling much better about the decision to spend the night in a real bed. The place was so empty that his concern about others seeing Carter's horn felt overly cautious. He smiled to himself, feeling the crisp touch of the AC unit humming to itself. Danielle and Roger had traded positions. While he had been in the shower, she had gone to bed early. She had climbed under the blankets and was still sleeping. Her chest rose and fell, unafraid.

Roger was just about to climb into bed as well, but he looked up. His eyes quickly scoured the room. James still sat at the end of the empty bed, but Carter was not in the room.

4

Roger felt his heart driving against his chest. How could they both be so stupid? He ran into the hallway, looking in both directions. It was empty. He turned to go off in search of Carter, but the door behind him opened, and James stood there. He looked to be ready for bed. He stood there, blinking into the hall light.

"Dad?" said James. Roger made a decision and took off quickly down the hallway.

"Stay here," said Roger. He could already feel a lump forming in his throat. They couldn't possibly be the only ones staying at the motel. How far did Carter go from the room? Fear was at his chest. A horrible image of Carter standing by the road waving at passing cars formed in Roger's head. The headlights would shine on his forehead. His horn would be exposed. And then his son would be taken to a science lab. The worry and fear of what the scientists would do to him rose in Roger. He imagined them cutting into his head with scalpels, extracting what they could for study. Then, they would discard his cadaver. He blinked and bit down on the thought that clouded his mind. The horn had to be kept secret. It was something that he had to make sure was never exposed to the world. Roger ran down the hallway.

He did not see any sight of Carter. He heard someone moving behind him. He stopped and turned around. There, running along behind him, was his younger son, James. Roger couldn't even bring himself to tell James to go back to the room. There was a beast awake in him. How could they have both been so stupid?

Roger ran down the hall, and James followed him outside. Roger looked both ways. He scanned the parking lot. Carter was nowhere in sight.

"Carter!" called Roger. He stood in the middle of the parking lot. He spun around, franticly scanning the evening air. The sky had slipped into twilight. The strong shadows lay across the world like faceless bodies left to die in fields. Their breaths smoking and blocking out the sky. To the west, a golden band still hung above the dark hand of night. It hung like a halo suspended above the shadows. The sky looked to be like an enormous bag filling with smoke from the burning world. It was a hot, warm night, fragrant with sweet wind.

Roger did not notice the smells or hear the sounds of cars driving along the road. He did not feel the wind, the heat on his body. He was untouched by everything that night. His heart rumbled in his chest as though it was having difficulty keeping up. There was something he did feel; however, it was more than fear or worry. It was something that was hidden in plain sight. Roger felt it like a train racing full speed towards a door. For some reason, he felt he had stepped through this door, and was now looking this train full in the face. Its headlight blinding and hot like the eye of a magnifying glass, a hot lance of sun. He felt it penetrate him, burn him, leaving nothing but a trail of smoke and ash for one to follow. He felt helpless to the terrors of that night.

It was the same way he had felt when Carter's forehead split. Powerless to the situation, unable to help, unable to stop the pain. Roger took a hard breath through his nose. He caught the faint hint of Carter's voice. A child laughter on the breeze. High and pitched above the roof of the motel.

A short hill near the motel rose softly, and there at its top was what looked to be a small playground. Through the shadows, he saw movement. He heard the sound of feet across wood planks. His heart continued to jump and stutter. It leaped into his throat, and he ran off towards the playground, fearing the worst.

A nearby lamppost clicked on, sensing the approaching night. Roger could only hope Carter had listened to their warnings and had kept his head covering on. He also knew his son was forgetful and he had complained about having to wear the hat for some time. Especially on the hottest days in the minivan. He wondered if when Danielle had said they needed a vacation that had sent the wrong message. They would never be able to truly let their guard down. Not until the horn was removed from his son's head. Only after the cut healed and the scar faded would they be able to have any true sense of peace.

Looking through the darkness, Roger caught sight of Carter high up on the jungle gym. He was laughing, preparing to go down the slide. Roger relaxed a little when he saw no one else was around. He managed to smile at the thought that, despite having a horn growing out of his head, Carter could still laugh. Not everything was as bleak as it seemed. He watched Carter come down the slide, all smiles and laughter. The hat was not on his head, and in the dark, the horn looked to have extended even further out.

"Carter," said Roger. The sight of the horn in the darkness gave a hard edge to Roger's fatherly tone. Carter's laughter was cut dead as he looked up and saw his father standing there.

"Get inside now!" said Roger. His stomach turned. He stood rigid, looking down at Carter until the boy was up and moving in the direction of the motel. Ever since the horn had started to grow, ever since he had felt its presence bubbling and pushing against the roof of his son's skull, he had hated it. Roger did not follow after Carter. The horn made his own stomach fill with dread. The sooner they got rid of it, the sooner it would be out of his mind. He looked around in the dark, assuming James had given up on following him and just returned to the room.

They could have no more slip-ups. There would be no more relaxing, not until the horn was removed. There was a cough, and Roger looked over. He felt his body run cold. Had Carter not been alone out here? Had the darkness not been enough to hide the growth on his forehead? Worry began to grow in him, and he felt it spin like a terrible, cold maelstrom. His eyes narrowed, and he scoured the darkness.

Not far from the jungle gym was a picnic table. Roger stood still, staring dubiously at the table. Had there actually been someone there? He tried to bring the sound of the cough back to his mind. It had been so abrupt that he wasn't even sure if he had heard the sound at all. Still, he did not move from his spot. The nearby lamppost gave just enough light for him to make out the legs of the bench. He took a step, moving slowly towards it. His feet did not make a sound as he approached the table. As he went, his mind turned the sound over and over. The thing was starting to swell. It was starting to glow like a living ember steadily burning hotter and hotter until engulfed in flame. There was another cough, and Roger froze.

Now that he was closer to the source, he could start to make out someone sleeping on the bench in the darkness. The chill of worry and fear swept through him. He continued to stand there as if frozen in time. As if all the clocks had stuttered and stopped their relentless march. Many thoughts flooded Roger in that moment. All of it felt to be pulling him toward the terrible act. It was like he was wadding through the darkness, and suddenly, he felt clawed hands reaching up, grabbing him. Pulling, dragging him to the depths. In that moment, he felt helpless. They could not risk the man telling anyone about the boy with the horn. Even if the man had retold it in a dream. They had been too careful so far. Then, Roger felt something in him ignite. He felt his body rise with anger and fire.

He moved closer to the slumbering man. He listened to the rise and fall of his chest. He timed his own heartbeat to the draw and pull of air. He didn't know if he could do it, but the chance and risk were too much not to. The man suddenly shot upright and opened his eyes. He pointed at Roger, and in a voice that was not his own but belonging to a woman who had cursed Roger pronounced,

"Cursed! A dread curse! The horn will grow until it burns with fire! Then you will die!" He threw himself on top of the sleeping man. His hands felt like stone as he took the man by the throat. The sleeping man woke from his dream. He screamed and bellowed in that terrible voice like a horrible blood moon. Like a forest in the distance consumed by flame. The sleeping man struggled and fought, but Roger's hatred was too strong. He did not relent. He continued to squeeze and shake. His arms were lengths of rope being pulled taught like a hangman's noose. The sleeping man had been sentenced to death. Roger panted in the darkness. Night looked to have strengthened. There was no moon that night, and the stars shone dully high above. Roger felt his arms slacken. He was still breathing hard. The blood in his body pounded in his ears. His chest felt like it was going to explode.

He steadied his breathing and listened to the man's chest. There was no heartbeat. His hands felt unwilling to release their hold. Slowly, he managed to open his hands, but they still trembled with the act of killing. All at once, he felt a hard pinch in his gut. Had he acted too hastily? Had his verdict been too quick? He felt the accusing eye of someone nearby, and he felt uncomfortable standing near the dead man. The adrenalin in his body left him feeling antsy. Insects scurrying under skin. He was a rotten house with termites and roaches infesting every nook and cranny, slowly devouring him from the inside.

Despite having slowed his breath. He still trembled with each intake. The cold feeling of his blood pooling in his fingertips did not go away. Roger remained a statue, unable to turn away from the man's pain-stricken face. A head wind started to blow, and Roger swayed unable to turn.

It was then that James appeared. He approached his father cautiously.

"Dad," said James, speaking below a whisper. Roger felt the strength in his legs give out, and he sat on the ground. James walked towards his father.

"How long were you here?" said Roger. He spoke, looking down into his hands. They were on the edge of the lamppost light.

"Are we going to live in the car again?" James moved closer to Roger and sat down next to his father.

"We are, but it will be fun. I promise. Nothing bad will happen to you."

"Or to Carter and mom?"

"Yes, I promise nothing bad will happen to any of you." The headwind continued to blow and sweep over them. Roger and James sat in the darkness, listening to the wind and the storm that was fast approaching.

5

Roger hid the body of the sleeping man and returned to their room. His mind was too full of worry. In the morning, they would have to leave quickly. They would have to get back into the minivan, and they would have to get as far away from the motel as they could. For many hours, he simply listened to Danielle's breathing. He figured letting her enjoy the innocent rest would be best before he broke the news to her. It could wait until morning. At some point, he must have settled into a dreamless sleep.

This nightmare was his making. He thought back to the events of the night before the horn. He struggled with sleep. He struggled to feel comfortable in the bed, resting beside his wife. Everything felt irritating. In the early hours of first light, Roger gave up on sleep. He decided to make use of the hot shower one last time before everyone else stirred from their slumbers. He knew no amount of heat could burn him of the guilt that was steadily growing in him. He had done what he could to keep them safe and protect Carter. Maybe someday, they would all be able to take a real vacation.

When he was done with his shower, he found Danielle waking from her sleep.

"I have to tell you something. Get dressed," said Roger. Danielle was out of bed. She stretched and took a deep breath through her nose.

"Can we stay one more night?" she asked.

"We need to get going. Carter was outside last night." Roger explained everything that happened, and Danielle did not say a word. She listened, her mouth partly open, eyes wide in disbelief.

"Let's let the kids eat breakfast," said Danielle.

"Be quick. I'll get things ready," said Roger.

Danielle took James and Carter down to get breakfast after putting the beanie cap back on his head. Roger went out to the office. He checked out of the motel. The old man behind the counter said nothing about reports of violence or anyone turning up missing. The more he talked with the clerk, the more his palms started to sweat. He resisted the urge to ask for the bathroom again and stepped outside the office.

Roger paced the parking lot. His gaze naturally fell to a stand of trees near the property's edge. He decided to walk back up to the playground and make sure, now that morning was coming, if there were any signs of struggle from last night's events. Even in the daylight, the spot still felt stained with blood. He already regretted killing the man, but there was no way of knowing how much he had seen. Roger's hands flexed like they were remembering, reliving the sensation of closing around the sleeping man's throat. He shivered at the thought of the voice and the warning it gave.

He swept his feet across the dirt, blotting out any trace of the act. As Roger stood by the bench, head turned toward the trees. He wondered how long James had been watching from the shadows. He wished they had left without breakfast. Morning had done nothing to calm his nerves. If anything, he felt more exposed in the morning light, like a beating heart in a chest that had been cut into. The ribs removed, so that all that is left is the thud of organ against loose skin.

He was still standing by the bench when he spotted Danielle and the kids entering the parking lot. He went to the brown minivan, and the four climbed inside without a word. James did not look up from his feet as he climbed into the back with his brother. They were moving once more. The minivan had been waiting for them with its familiar smells. The harsh temperature lingered still, making the interior musty, wet, and oppressive.

A bitter silence was at their throats, filling their stomachs with stones, filling each of them with a terrible weight. Roger looked out at the road before them. He blinked. The sleeping man's face rose in him. He felt it like a chilling scream ravaging his gut. Even after the motel fell away to the distance, he felt the presence of the dead man on his mind. His eyes constantly flickered between the road and the rearview mirror. He was watching James in the backseat.

He was so young. Too young to have to stare death in the face. Death was one of those concepts that you feel like a ghostly wind. It passes by with its hint of summer, of fresh fruits and green leaves browned and dried by the summer sun. You see the effects of death long before you understand what it means. You see it in the changes in the seasons, in how your dog is no longer so wild. The way your parents start to shrivel and shrink.

The road was long, and every mile they put between the motel felt like a mile closer to their journey's end. In time, Roger continued to feel the noose-like concern that someone might find the sleeping man's body. He could feel it building. They would soon be near the border, and all they would have to worry about was making it the rest of the way to the doctor. He looked up in the rearview mirror. He was growing steadily excited to be rid of the horn. He grimaced, remembering the warning given before he committed the act. He had to silence the voice. He had done what he had to do to protect them all. And he knew he would do it again to keep them safe. He only wished James had not been present to see the fierce cut to his eyes. He wished James had just stayed inside.

Carter was scratching and picking at the hard skin around his horn. Roger could make out the sound of his fingers rubbing against the strange carapace skin. He could see flakes of it rubbing off like a snake shedding its skin.

"Dad, it itches," said Carter. He was digging in with both sets of fingers. His nails scraped the skin with an incurable itch. They kept driving, but after another minute or two,

Danielle pulled the car over as Carter continued to scratch. Roger jumped out and climbed into the backseats. The minivan started moving again. Carter was drawing blood as he scratched now.

"Carter, are you alright?" said Roger. James did not look at his father now. He looked down at his feet. Roger could almost feel the fragility of his son's mind. It was like ghosts were lying across the backseats. Swallowing the three of them. The tips of Carter's fingers were red and flecks of blood had stuck under each of his nails so that it looked like some ferocious animal had chewed at the tips of his fingers. Carter had pain written across his face.

"It'll be okay," said Roger.

"It feels hot," said Carter. He leaned forward, pulling his hair away from the protruding horn. Roger saw that Carter had scratched himself raw. Here and there were tracks of fingernails leaving patchwork scrapes of blood. How long had Carter been scratching at his forehead? Roger delicately moved towards the horn. He went slowly, not wanting to have Carter pull away. If Carter did let him touch it, it would be the first time since the horn appeared. Since the time he had tried to cut the horn out of his son's head. The memory of Carter's screaming stirred in Roger.

"Are you sure it's the horn?" said Roger. He tried to keep the concern from his voice, but this was the first time Carter had ever mentioned the horn being hot. Carter nodded with a pain-stricken expression as though he were sick.

The pain felt like a constant in the boy's life. So long as the strange growth was there, Carter would always be in pain. That was why they were doing what they were doing. It was all to care for Carter and ensure James and Carter were safe. He lightly took the horn in his hands.

It felt alien. It was a foreign object that felt so out of place, like a bone that has broken and healed incorrectly so that it now curves in the wrong direction. Legs that only bend backward, an arm that curves out. It's familiar but so drastically different that it twists your stomach into metal wiring that is wound so tight it's nothing more than a knot of wires and useless metal. The horn did indeed feel hot to the touch. It was like a slab of stone baking in a summer sun. The heat rising and permeating from the surface.

Roger brushed the hair of his son out of the way of the blood on his forehead.

"Would you like us to stop?" said Roger.

Carter nodded, and Roger looked out the window for a moment. They were on a stretch of backroad, the sun beating down, and heat rose off the asphalt. He replayed the Deadman's final words: "Cursed! A dread curse! The horn will grow until it burns with fire! Then you will die!"

"Try not to itch. We'll stop in the next town," said Roger. He was worried all the stopping was getting them into more trouble than it was worth. Roger moved to the middle seats and sat behind Danielle. If they had never stopped at the motel, if they had just kept driving, then there would be no dead man hidden in the bushes. There would still be the woman. She was in his memory like a fire in the night on a mountainside. A blazing sun cresting a mountain range. The thought sickened him, but he knew she would always be there like a stain he could never hope to wash away.

Roger closed his eyes and rested for a moment. He languished in thought. His memories felt like they were persecuting him. Like he was a guilty man being shouted at from the juror's box. He wrestled with the feeling. For the moment, Carter had stopped his scratching. However, every now and then, Roger heard him groan like he was dying in a field. Each time, it sent a pang through him and twisted his stomach. Even though he had thought about stopping in the next town, Roger was reluctant to stop. The last time they stopped, he had killed a man. What if someone else saw Carter? What if someone else witnessed the terrible horn? Would he have to go on killing people? Continue to feel the breath in his hands squeezed in his fingers, seeing the last painful shape of their mouth right before they die?

He grimaced.

"I think we might be about to enter a town," said Danielle. She spoke over her shoulder at her husband. The horn had felt hot, and Roger knew Carter was suffering.

"We'll need to stop in town," said Roger, leaning forward to whisper in Danielle's ear. Roger went back to the backseats and was checking on Carter. Roger couldn't tell if the horn was growing in that moment or if it was his mind playing tricks on him. The horn looked like it was giving off a radio wave, a heat that seemed to rise and transmit a signal. Roger placed his hands around the horn. This time, he felt the heat pushing against his fingers.

"Are you alright, Carter? How do you feel?" He tried to keep the concern in his voice from spiking, but there was too much worry and fear rolling around in his gut. His voice trembled. Roger desperately wished he could do something to ease his son's suffering. It didn't seem fair that the horn should also make him feel so ill. Having a horn sticking out of your head should be enough, thought Roger.

They were all silent as they entered the next town. There was a sense of space like so many of the northern New England towns. Two roads had crossed and people had just decided to build a town in the middle. Without being prompted, Carter and James lay down on the floor. James still had not spoken since the night at the motel. Roger helped to spread the blanket over their bodies. The kids wriggled and moved like buried things rising to the surface like sickness ravaging a body. Like famine and disease spreading through a country. Trembling like a ripple on still water.

Roger turned away from them. The idea brought the sight of worms to his mind. He could see them like he was still standing over the sleeping man. He knew that in a few days, perhaps a week or more, the worms and flies would swarm the body. Then, someone might stumble upon the smell. In his mind, he knew someone might scream at the sight of the melted face. The blood drained from the body. There would be the pungent smell of death, the kind that reveals how rotten people are on the inside. He shook his head and tried to turn from the thought.

Carter still complained about how hot his horn felt. His voice was high and whiny, full of tears being pinned back.

"I'll go in," said Roger. He pointed out the window to a hardware store. "There's some things we'll need." Danielle looked at her husband. He could see her face twisting as though forming around a word. As if she might express something, but Danielle did not speak. She simply pulled the minivan over, and Roger got out without her bringing the car to a full stop. He was alone once more. He looked around as if checking for something.

He entered the hardware store. For some time, he wished they had had a way to measure the growth of the horn. He was beginning to feel his mind becoming heavy with questions. He was becoming more suspicious. Had the woman – had she truly cursed him? Had Edna, or Lucile, or Linda, whatever her name had truly been, had her Latin been better than she let on? What could he not remember? He clenched his jaw as he tried to force his mind to lift the fog that had been her wine, that had been the secret, and the cover of night. But it was like trying to be able to see to the end of the galaxy. Forcefully willing your vision to go on, to be able to pierce a little further, a little deeper.

Roger stood in one of the aisles, lost in thought. It took him a moment, but he managed to shake the feeling of that night. He knew he had to focus. The fact that they had stopped again after having stopped for a night in a motel. He almost felt the need to look over his shoulder. It was like a slow, lumbering monster weighed down by weeds and thick branches, a swamp monster rising from the depths of the lake. Dragging its body on shore in a slow pursuit.

He shook his hands and shuffled his feet. Roger bought a measuring tape and some other odds and ends. He picked up a set of tools because he had started to wonder what would happen if the engine on the six-hundred-dollar minivan were to quit. He also purchased a hammer. With his order placed in a bag, he left the hardware store.

Next, they found a pharmacy. Roger made his way along the aisles. He knew no pill or syrup would remove a horn from your head, but he wished there could be such a thing. He bought a handful of different labeled and colored children's cold and flu medicines. He chose a best mom ever card from the Mother's Day section of the greeting cards.

It was a miracle that they could all get along so well after days of being trapped in a hot minivan. Danielle was quick to find Roger after he finished his shopping. She looked at him as he opened the door and climbed in.

"What's wrong?" said Roger.

"I'll tell you once we get out of town."

6

Danielle was silent and did not attempt to explain what was wrong. Even after they had left the town and were making good time along the road, she remained silent. Her body was strong, like it was cast of stone. She almost appeared to be ignoring Roger and his concerned look in the passenger seat.

"I got you this," said Roger. He reached into the pharmacy bag and took out the Mother's Day card. "You've been doing a lot." Danielle softened her gaze from the road.

Her jaw unclenched, and her features slackened as she looked at the card.

"While you were gone," she said. "A report came over the radio. Seems the person from the motel had a wife and kids. I wish I could remember more of it." Her voice splintered as she bit down on the last word. "Roger, it's a big mess. This whole thing is one big mess!" Her voice sharply rose. She sniffed. "I've tried to stay calm this whole time. But I don't know. What are we going to do? Even if we get rid of this thing." She was suddenly deathly silent, wiping her face with a free hand.

The minivan started to drift towards the left lane, and Roger could hear the pistons and gears accelerating. A high-revving noise rose like the clicking teeth of a horrible monster. Like a churning stomach burning and bubbling. Danielle started to hit the steering wheel with her free hand. Her breath punctuated the anger in her chest. The strain had been on her since they first discovered the horn growing out of their son's head.

Then the pistons and the racing gears powered down, like the mind of a robot being forcefully shut off. The red electronic glow faded to an everlasting black, and the minivan rolled to a stop. They were in the middle of the left lane of the highway.

"What are you doing?" said Roger. "Is it the engine?" He made a move as though to reach into the bag from the hardware store. "Why didn't you pull over further?" There was an edge in his voice now. And it came out like a steel blade slicing into soft skin. Leaving a crude mark and drawing blood to follow in the wake of the slash. Danielle had both hands on the wheel. Several cars rushed past them. A tractor-trailer rumbled past and shook the minivan.

There was a break in the passing traffic.

"We have to move the car!" said Roger. There was no response from Danielle. Roger reached for the door. Danielle was unresponsive, as though blanketed in a momentary darkness of static electricity. He opened the car door and stepped into the middle of the highway. Pressing his body against the minivan, he edged his way around the vehicle, moving like a man standing on a ledge overlooking a high-rise. He edged all the way to the other side. He was at the back of the vehicle. He saw exhaust was still flowing from the tailpipe.

Before he threw his shoulder against the mass of metal, Roger realized the car was still working perfectly fine. The engine had not stopped working. There was still gas in the tank.

He went to the driver's side door. Danielle looked at him. She paused a moment, and her foot remained pressed on the brakes.

"Why are we stopped!" said Roger. He no longer tried to mask the edge in his voice. His blood boiled. The heat from the sun rose in waves around him. It was suffocatingly hot. The van would soon bake in the sun, set to roast on the black asphalt. The temperature inside would rise to three hundred, maybe to five hundred degrees. They would all burn inside. Why were they not moving? What was Danielle getting at? He ground his teeth, and his hands clenched, flexing like they were tightening around a sleeping man's throat. He had done it once before. He was starting to think he could do it again. Would this be the end of the line for them?

The smell of tar and heat was in his nose. His whole body quivered. There was a rotten, sour smell that rolled through the heat. It mingled with the hot temperature, stunk of time, and death. It was a summer candle melting in a blazing sun. A car shot by, and Roger felt the heat, the smell, and the rising waves shift a moment before bristling back into position.

"We need to talk," said Danielle at last.

"Let's get somewhere safe," said Roger, a little calmer now that Danielle was actually responding. His whole body was perspiring. Every inch of him felt coated in salt, sweat, and heat. It was like he had been dipped into a vat of melted silver. The heat stuck to every inch of him. "What the hell are we doing in the middle of the highway?" said Roger. He started pacing. If he stood still too long, it felt like a magnifying glass hanging over him.

"There was never a chance to talk," said Danielle. How could she be so calm, thought Roger. They could be obliterated at any moment by a car drifting too far to the left. Or if some eighteen-wheeler were to pass at just the wrong time. They would be bugs on a windshield. Danielle had kept her hands on the wheel, and aside from opening her window, she had remained with both hands on the wheel.

"Would you pull the car over?" Danielle nodded and, slowly, she pulled the car as far as she could over to the side of the road. Then, they were both out of the minivan. Both standing on the stretch of highway, being cooked in the sun. The smell of death and melted rubber was thick in their noses, like foul-smelling water that had been stagnant and overgrown with green things. Like a body swelled in the ocean and split down the middle. Guts opened and spilling rancid seawater. So much deflated skin wrapped around chewed bones.

"I didn't think you were capable of killing someone." Her voice sounded tired, drained of energy. A dog panting in the doorway. She moved towards him. "I need to know since we never had a chance to talk about it. We're in this together."

"Of course," he said. And he meant it, too.

"We've been through a lot so far. I'm just." She paused as if the words had melted like ice on her tongue like they were reluctant to leave her mouth. "I'm worried about Carter and James." She looked at the minivan. The boys would no doubt be uncomfortable stewing in the back of the car, even with the windows open. A few more cars shot past them, but they went unnoticed.

"We'll do what we can," said Roger. He brought a hand to his brow, shielding the sun from his eyes. "We'll be at the border soon. Things will turn out okay, you'll see." He meant this, too. He looked away from Danielle and absently scanned the sky. There were no clouds to give any shade. The sun was unrelenting. "Let's get out of this heat," he said.

As they climbed back into the vehicle, Roger knew they had only grazed the surface of what they would need to talk about. He knew they would eventually need to let themselves be exposed like cadavers awaiting autopsies. Skeletons stripped of skin and muscle.

7

The boys were both still in the backseats. Danielle had given
each of them a bottle of water when Roger got out of the car.
They were both quiet. Now, the entire minivan felt like a
ghostship. The boys in the back did not make a sound. There
was no protesting or poking at each other's elbows. Roger and
Danielle were both sweating and silent in the front seats. The
silence lay over them like the spirit of a dead man. Like visiting
the home of someone who has just died. Climbing the stairs that
for so many years only knew one weight, and going to stand in

the now empty bedroom. To breathe the same air that had only touched one set of lungs and had sustained only one person no longer there. The talk on the highway had done little to ease their hearts and their minds. Carter still had his horn. No one spoke. They barely moved. They were soldiers left panting in a blood-soaked field. Their tongues pinned to their mouths.

They were off the highway and nearing the northern border. It would be the last time they would need to fear someone seeing past Carter's disguise. Border crossing was never enjoyable, even if you didn't have a child with a horn growing in his head. They had to hope that the border officers would not lift the cap from their son's head. They were both young enough that Roger hoped it would be just a matter of handing four passports over before awaiting a verdict.

He had the passports in his hands and was shuffling them like a deck of cards. Nearing the border gate, Roger stopped his shuffling. He flipped open the one of Carter. The picture was from earlier that year. Before his forehead had suddenly split. He looked at the smiling face, all lips and no teeth. The kind of childlike smile that makes a parent's heart bleed. They parked the car, calculating fuel left in the tank. Roger placed the passports in his pockets, and Danielle and Roger glanced at one another.

"Carter, please do not touch your hat," said Roger. James was the last to climb out of the hot minivan.

"Are we ready?" asked Danielle. She and Roger knew they would never be ready to face the challenge of getting past border patrol with their sons. But the roads had run their course. Still, rolling around in their gut was the sense that they were all woefully unprepared. Like a magician attempting a death-defying trick for the first time. There was so much room for error. And the difference between success and failure meant the difference between life and death.

Their lungs felt knotted, and Roger and Danielle took short, shallow breaths. Carter kept his hands at his sides like imitating a toy soldier. James was still ghost-like ever since the incident at the motel. He had not spoken a word since then. Roger looked to the border. His eyes jumped between the guards. They weren't dressed like police officers, but he was certain his wife had the creeping feeling of ice at her throat. It was almost enough to turn them away.

Roger felt a hand tug at his shirt. He looked down and saw Carter standing beside him. Carter had his head tilted back and was staring up at his father. He silently waved to him. Roger bent down, and Carter put his mouth next to Roger's ear.

"My horn itches," said Carter.

"Here," said Roger. He put a hand on the hot ground and went down on one knee.

"Here you go," said Roger. He put his fingers under the cap and gently scratched the horn. It still felt hot, but Roger saw Carter nod. "Are we ready to go in?" Carter nodded with his whole body. Roger stood, and Carter pulled the hat a little lower over his head. They made their way towards the border. Once inside, both Roger and Danielle answered all the questions. James and Carter hung back a few feet from their parents and watched as they were inspected.

"Just spending a little vacation in Toronto," said Roger.

"Toronto's a little distance from here, eh?" replied the border officer, looking over the four passports. "Those are your kids?" He pointed at the pictures of Carter and James, then to the children themselves.

"They are," said Danielle. "James and Carter." James was looking down at his feet. While Carter had a puzzled look of concentration on his face. His hands were dangerously close to reaching for his forehead. It was truthfully only a matter of a few minutes, but each passing second felt like grinding gears in Roger's stomach. The official stamped Roger and Danielle's passports. He still held Carter and James's. He tilted the pictures to the light.

"James," said the border officer. James flinched but did not look up. The teeth of the gears were now irritably grinding against one another. There was friction, heat, and a collision. Roger grimaced.

"James?" said Danielle. He didn't pick his head up. "We're sorry. We've been in the car for a while," she explained. The passports were stamped and handed back to Roger. They practically ran back to the minivan. Even though it would still be stuffy and smell like sweaty bodies, it felt safe. It was a feeling of drifting in the ocean where everything was uncomfortable. The abrasive salt stripping the skin like clawed hands. The sun burning your neck and drying what's left of you. So much tumultuous uncertainty, but still clinging to this bit of driftwood to keep you alive.

Danielle drove past the gate. The tension in her shoulders and neck left the moment they passed through. Roger still looked around. He couldn't shake the feeling that things would not always be so easy. Something inexplicable rose in him. The troubling gears were freely spinning, attached to nothing.

"One less thing to worry about," said Roger. Danielle gave a weak smile and rubbed at her eyes.

"How are you both doing back there?" said Danielle. There was no response from the back of the minivan. Both children had their tongues cut from their mouths. They were faded like ghosts in sunlight. Slowly disappearing to mist over a hallowed land. Rising, floating in midair. Roger and Danielle both looked in the rearview mirror. Their sons were still sitting in the back of the minivan. Watching them, like they always had, the fragility of those looks was glass under mounting pressure. There were hairline cracks that were starting to form. Drawn as though by a single finger etching spider webs into the innocence that was the young ages of Carter and James.

Roger looked away from the mirror. He blinked. The gears in him spun wildly like car wheels after an accident.

"Do you want to turn in early?" suggested Roger. He opened the passenger mirror. The bags under his eyes were deep, dark bruises. His complexion was pale. He tenderly touched the spots under his eyes. "They've had it rough." He leaned over to whisper to his wife.

"Yeah, that sounds nice," said Danielle. They drove into the early afternoon. After the day's heat broke, they came across a remote field. They had been passing nothing but open, flat lands for some time. Sparse and remote clearings seemed to be all that existed between the eastern and middle section of

Canada. Interspersed now and then, there was a small general store or coffee shop. But for the most part, it was all relatively undeveloped wilderness.

The worry of the dead man being found was now a distant thought in Roger's mind. It was as though the man had always been dead, but no, Roger knew this was not true. He knew the trouble might still be there when they came back to the States. For now, he pushed it to the back of his mind, knowing they all had more important worries bearing down on them.

They opened all the doors of the musty, heat-filled van. It was so full of travel and wear. The thing was like a wounded creature lumbering alone through the woods. So far, it had served them well enough to manage the lengthy days of travel. Roger could practically hear the bones of this enormous animal crying out as its strained muscles frayed like unraveling ropes. The legs quivered on unsure footing. Fatigue and famine eating away any of the healthy tissue. Only the vital organs remained functioning. The indomitable spirit dragging its shackles across the land. They, too, had kept going.

James and Carter lay spread-eagled on the ground. They even let Carter take his hat off. He ran his fingers through his hair and scratched his horn. The feeling of the afternoon sun on his scalp made him smile. The temperature was perfect. Not too hot, but not too cold either. A light breeze touched the grass and ruffled their hair, playfully tugging at their shirts. They inhaled the deep smell of wild land. The hint of hidden water seeping from the ground. They could not get enough of the clean, fresh air. They turned their faces to the glancing sun, rubbed their faces, and pinched their eyes. The world a glow with the afternoon summer sun that hangs there, unwilling to set. Roger hoped that they could stay in that moment forever. He and Danielle set a blanket on the ground and were lying side by side. As they both lay there, he realized she felt like a stranger to him. They had been drifting apart for so long.

He had been staying out later than he should. Always returning after she had fallen asleep. They lay there dreaming. Roger's mind fell back on all the terrible things he'd done. The way he had failed as a husband, as a father. He thought back to the birthdays he'd missed. He'd broken promises to her, the kids, or to both. The night he spent with Lucile was on display in his mind. His jurors sneered at him. They threw things at him, chanting in his mind their verdict. Guilty, they shouted! Guilty! Again and again, Roger heard the voices in his chest and his mind. His heart tightened as if shutting down just a little as if demonstrating its power to suddenly stop beating.

He shifted his weight to his back and tried to readjust his position without disturbing Danielle, who was lying beside him. He stood. He stepped away from her. Her body curved, sleeping on her side like a slender blade. Her dreams full of thoughts of happiness and moonshine. The sun had relinquished its hold on the sky and dropped to the horizon. The sky burned. Roger felt the heat touch him. He had managed not to wake the others. They were all so tired. They deserved sleep and a chance to rest in the open air.

For too long, they had been bodies sealed away in a tomb. They had breathed the same stale, musty air, their brains running low on good oxygen. Roger made his way to the brown minivan which sat and watched them sleeping like it was a bear that had crept up behind them in the woods. Something about the way it looked at them. The way it appeared so out of place made Roger shiver. He placed a hand over the engine, feeling the heat rise as though it was panting. Something was in Roger's head. As he stood by the minivan, he looked out over his sleeping family. He thought it wasn't fair that they should all suffer. He guessed much about the actions of his night with Lucile. He had given up on trying to scavenge another name. He couldn't be bothered to know whether it was her name. He could not understand why the curse had not given him a horn. It was unfair, he thought, to punish his sons. To punish his wife.

His jurors were rushing towards him. They charged the witness stand. In his mind, he did not flinch from the fire in their eyes. The hatred in their hearts. He felt he deserved it all. He let his chin rest against his chest and stared down into his feet as the sun set and twilight came.

Roger turned his glance several times. His eyes felt jumpy like he was being stalked. Something that moved quickly and surrounded him in a blur of movement and teeth.

Roger remained by the minivan. He could not bring himself to sleep by the others. He sat in the driver's seat for a while, hands on the steering wheel. He reached for the keys twice but couldn't bring himself to start the engine.

He could sense another dark presence like an eye sweeping over the land, scouring for something lost. Then Lucile was in the passenger seat. She reached out and touched the back of his hand. Roger held his breath. His hands gripped the wheel as she drew a line up his arm. It was almost sensual, like it had been that night before everything went wrong. She reached a hand underneath his shirt, and he could feel her tracing some intricate design on his skin. She started to hiss, and her touch started to burn. Roger sweated.

"Cursed, a dread curse," she said. Then she was gone. Roger sat shaking in the driver's seat. He reached for his shirt and looked at the spot she had touched. There was no mark left that he could see. He looked out in the deep twilight evening. The world appeared tranquil, quiet. No sounds but the rush of wind through grass and the hum of crickets. He made up his mind that he had simply dosed off and imagined it.

"Do you all need help?" asked a voice. Roger's head shot up. A flash of danger came to him. As though a bolt of lightning struck the ground inches away. It was hot, burning, and brilliant light. Roger listened a moment, then reached for the hammer in the glove box. He touched the handle, letting his fingers wrap around it. The voice hit him like a steel pipe in complete darkness. Making his way from the road was a man. He stood fifteen, maybe ten feet away. Roger got out of the van. He was helpless, unable to speak. He felt the spike of anger that had touched him back at the motel. Was he going to have to kill this man, too? He was still moving towards them. Roger felt his blood rise in him. A voice shouted at him to kill. It would be better than last time. It would be easier. There would be no hesitation. He would have to do something now.

8

"Go away! Go away!" yelled Roger. His voice spitting lava at the man. Now, he was the hunter. The man turned and ran. Roger chased after him. There was a delight in it now. A kind of adrenaline. It heightened his senses. The man saw the look in Roger's eye. He had been that close. It was the look of a man no longer afraid of what might happen. A man with nothing to lose. The man tripped and fell. Roger was on top of him now. Hammer raised. The other fought back, swinging his body side to side, doing everything to keep Roger off him. Roger gripped the hammer. He swung but missed. It stuck in the ground. His heart was beating out of his chest. The carnal awakening took over, and Roger became a blood-crazed wolf. He punched and hit as hard as he could. The man's eyes rolled back into his head, showing only the exposed creamy white undersides of his eyeballs.

Roger could hear the man's heart beating in his chest. He pulled the hammer out of the ground. His fingers flexed greedily at the weight in his hand. They trembled with delight in the act. He was on his knees, straddling this man. It was just like how he had been when he killed The Sleeping Man. It all felt so familiar. The heat in his face, the anger in his eyes, the quiver of his muscles as they clenched down. The coming death. He raised the hammer.

Roger was pushed. His fingers slipped as he was knocked to his side, dropping the hammer. The other man gasped. Roger blinked, still unsure of what had knocked him off his victim.

"Roger! What are you doing?" said Danielle. She was now standing over both of the men on the ground. She looked at them. "Go now!" The man scrambled to his feet and looked at Danielle, panting, still dizzy. She stared at him. He turned and ran back to his car.

"Why did you stop me?" said Roger, getting to his feet. His arms hung limp at his sides. He couldn't bring himself to look at his wife.

"Do you think he saw anything? It's getting dark. You can't keep killing people, Roger. It has to stop," said Danielle. Her face was all stone and harsh angles. Even in the dim light, Roger sensed the scowl on her face.

"What if he tells the police?"

"We'll deal with it. I doubt he will," said Danielle.

Danielle turned and began moving back to where Carter and James were sleeping.

"Danielle, wait. I have to tell you something." His voice was weak. Roger could not keep the tremble from his tongue. It spread throughout his body until he was feeling the electric shock of terror pulsing through him. His muscles flexed and relaxed in rapid succession. The last bit of life the electric chair gives to a psychotic killer, like the demon within is being exorcised.

"Hold on," said Danielle. She turned around and started towards the minivan. It still stood watch. Roger let out a strained breath. He probed his body with his mind. Maybe it would be better to leave the issue for another night. His hands felt like they had been left in a freezer. The joints stiff and unwilling to curl.

"We should probably get out of here," said Roger. Danielle had gathered blankets from the back of the minivan.

"We can let them rest a little longer," said Danielle.

"Twenty minutes," said Roger.

The burning colors of red, orange, and pink had silently disappeared. Streaks of deep plum lay like ribbons in the sky. There was a feeling of expanse in the twilight. Like a never-ending road. Fifteen minutes later, the sky succumbed to night. It spread slowly like ink seeping into paper. There were no stars just yet. But Roger wished he might see one in the sky before they had to leave. A few minutes later, they were waking Carter and James. They clenched their eyes, clinging to the final glimpses of a wonderful summer dream. The golden summer smells like the last ride at a carnival fair. It's all lights, screams in your core. It's excitement. It's sadness, and it's sorrow. You try and hold it in your hand. But the moment you try and look at it, it slips out of your fingers. Roger looked into the sky. He strained his eyes into the shiny, jet night. He silently hoped things would not always be this way.

"I'm not getting in!" said James. His voice was disconnected from him in the night. He stopped moving.

"James, we have to keep going," Danielle said softly.

"No!" James moved away. His feet made a barely audible sound as he backed away from the minivan.

"James," said Roger. He moved toward his youngest son.

"Don't grab my neck!" shouted James. James ran. The minivan now held more terror in the young child's mind. Roger pursued. James screamed and ran. The Night was so dark that Roger had to guess by James's screams where the boy was.

"James, come back," said Danielle. Roger stopped his chasing. The dark was too strong.

"I'm not going!" said James. His high-pitched voice punctured the air. James started screaming, a throat-tearing, bloody scream. The sound lashed out at Roger and Danielle each time James took a ragged breath and wailed. Something was cloying in their minds. Like a killer with a knife standing over you, only the moon to illuminate his wide, grinning face. All around nothing but darkness to fill the space as you wake, scream, and scream.

James's tantrum screams became infrequent. The gaps of silence filled in quickly, and soon, his cries were more tears than blood-curdling shouts. The stars overhead started to poke out like needles in fine cloth. A pale, grim moon shone, turning the world a ghostly silver. James sat on the ground in full tears. His arms holding his knees. His body heaved and swayed back and forth. They let him cry, Roger and Danielle watched their son.

After a while, James stopped his crying. He blinked and sniffed, and wiped at his face.

"How much further do we have to go?" asked James. He rose a little, still holding his knees tightly to his chest. In another moment, he was up and making his way towards the minivan.

"James, I wish you hadn't seen it, said Roger. "I promise I won't let anything bad happen to you. To any of you." They all climbed into the minivan. The engine was turned on, and they were moving once more.

9

The silence consumed them. Each felt a hand at his and her
throat. An icy grasp that had tightened considerably since they
had stopped for the brief rest. James's outburst left him tired,
and he was the first asleep in the back of the minivan. Danielle
and Roger wanted to put some miles between the spot where
Roger attacked The Approaching Man and them. Roger looked
out the window. His gaze at the trees with their shadows and
filled branches. He could still hear the sound of James's wails.
It wracked his heart and his chest.

Despite the decision to try and go to bed early, there was going to be little comfort that night. Roger rubbed the spots under his eyes. They felt like open sores. The bruises so deep and dark. He scratched at the backs of his hands. Roger put his fingers through his beard and sighed. He was just as tired if not more than when they had found the remote field to rest in sunlight.

Sadly, no sunset lasts forever. No summer never fades. The darkness is always there, burning at the edges like a dormant disease waiting to consume the body. There is no sorrow in death. Dying is only a slow process. When they had traveled what felt to be a safe distance away from the open field, they pulled over and shut off the car. James and Carter were both asleep. Their breathing mixed in the backseats, and it resonated through the small space.

"Nice to see James talking again," said Danielle, lying down as best she could. The smell of sunlight and the green of the field still hung in their noses. The scents of the long sunset filled their minds like an intoxicating perfume.

Roger's dreams were not filled with fields, wind, or sunlight. He slept on his side. He was in the gray middle ground of dreaming and consciousness when he started to feel as though smoke was filling the vehicle's cabin. He felt like someone was filling a room with cigar smoke or something was burning. He also could swear he felt something looking at him. Eyes wide, brimming with fire like a crazed devil. The gaze unsettled him. He opened his eyes, and there, in the back of the van, glowing like a piece of metal taken from a forge, he saw the horn on Carter's head.

It gave off a terrible red glow that looked like it could spark and take the whole family in a swift fire. It was strange and mesmerizing. The red light looked like a terrible pupil to a giant eye at first glance. It looked to flick its attention back and forth as Carter nodded his head in his dreams. It was surveying, looking between him and Danielle. Roger flinched at the thought. Was this how the horn grew? Was it growing now? Roger could not pull his attention away from the strange light. It gave off no heat but sent a chill through him like he was drowning in ice. He remembered the warning. It sent shockwaves through him.

Roger's eyes filled with that glow; his lower lip quivered. His breath stuck in his throat. All he could do was stare mouth agape. His heart trembled in his chest. Then, there was a flicker of light where Carter's eyes might be. Where they should be if he was a normal boy. It was as though the eyes had suddenly opened, red and enraged. At that moment, Carter was no more. Roger stared at the thing in the back of the van. The glowing horn like a lance of fire thrust at him. He reached for the door with a shaky hand.

The possibility of running filled his mind. In a moment, the thought of spilling out into the darkness, running, and leading the terrible monster away from the rest of them passed in his mind. He knew he would not make it far before the creature would burst from the windows and bound after him. The horn seeking him. Driving his heart to burst as the terrible eyes leered through the dark. He shuttered to think of the thing in the backseat, grinning like a devilish face at the window.

The thing in the back of the minivan looked squarely at Roger. It started to whisper in a voice that sounded like so much wind being pulled down a drain. The eyes all terror and fire. The horn now pulsed with a light that looked at him. Roger felt pure, cold terror rake through his insides.

He jumped awake. Roger blinked. His vision still blurry. His heart still trembled, and a large lump in his throat. He coughed. Gradually, his senses returned, and his mind focused on his surroundings. They were still in the minivan. He sat up in his seat. The memory of what he had seen staring at him in the back of the van still held terror in his mind. Roger wasn't sure if he could bring himself to look back and see if the monster was still watching him. He held his breath. Then turned and looked. Sleeping soundly in the back was Carter and James. Carter sounded a little louder while sleeping, but not enough to suggest he had been hissing at his father during the night. Roger let out the air in his lungs.

Danielle had parked the minivan on the edge of a road with a clearing and a small tree line. It was lush and green. However, here and there were patches of splotchy yellows from the lack of rainfall that year. There was movement from the stand of trees. A doe and her fawns stepped out on their long legs in the early morning. They were brown with flecks of white. Roger watched them walk out in the gray morning light. Their movements were tranquil like hearing water trickle through rocks. The fluidity of their motion, the calm, unafraid look in their eyes. It held serenity in it, and Roger watched and breathed, scarcely moving.

They passed just a few feet in front of the brown vehicle. The deer did not know the terror that had been transported all the way across the map. The brimming evil that rested in a sudden growth. The horn that had sprouted from his son's forehead. One of the younger deer had what appeared to be the start of a developing antler. The bone-white nub growing out of the creature's head. But here, it looked natural, like the animal would be incomplete without the sprouting bone.

Roger sat thinking back to the night when everything started. His mind quickly became submerged in thought. The night still weighed on his mind, like a thorn had been stuck in him and never removed. Left alone and allowed to slowly burrow deeper into him, pushing its way ever closer to his beating heart. He imagined the thorn driving through him like a stake into a vampire. He imagined it continuing to beat, now leaking blood. With each pound of his chest, a little more oozed out. He imagined his heart emptying itself, turning black, before becoming still as a hard chunk of stone. He closed his eyes until he saw spots form in the dark. The cold feeling did not relinquish. Roger opened his door and got out of the car. He stood just outside for a moment, surveying the landscape. It was flat and misty that morning. The gray sun reflected in the drifting clouds gave the impression of silver trapped in ice.

He frowned, rubbing his forehead. His mind sluggish and worn down from the days of intense scrutiny. He felt like yelling. He wanted to scream so loud that the trees would shake with his voice. He wanted to fill his throat with the sound of a deep, bellowing scream. He was being driven to the point of madness. He felt it like he was approaching the ledge of a high building. As though he had prepared himself to stare death in the face. What had Lucile done to him? He pinched and tugged at his forehead. Shaping his face in grotesque ways.

What was the purpose of all the pain he was bearing? Why was she tormenting him so? Roger walked to the tree line. He looked around. They were completely alone. The world washed in silver mist, like a ghostly breath smoking and filling a room. If it wasn't for the nearby road and the brown minivan, it would be possible to think that humans had never discovered this remote place. Or they had and just decided it wasn't worth settling down. The place was so remote. So empty of any kind of relevance to the rest of the world. It would be designed only to pass swiftly through. Yet, here it offered Roger and the rest of his sleeping family an opportunity to sleep. It allowed them to be nothing more than shadows in a world of light and sun.

Roger looked around one more time. He almost felt silly about what he was about to do. But there was no reason to feel squeamish about anything at this point in his life. He had killed a man and came close to killing a second. There was nothing left for him to be ashamed of. He pulled in a sharp draw of air, threw his head back, and screamed. He roared several times. Until it hurt his throat to do so.

10

Danielle woke to the sounds of Roger's hoarse cries. It jolted her awake. In a moment, she was out of the car and standing in the misty morning. She silently shut the door and stood perplexed, watching as her husband screamed by a stand of trees. She felt a quiver touch her face, and she half raised her hand to cover it. She watched Roger bellowing. She had known for some time about the difficulties in their marriage. The way Roger had been growing secretive. How he had been staying out late almost every night. It was something like pity, but not quite, that touched her in that moment. A passing emotion that had a bitter scent to it. It was the smell of her father's hand as he had held her before his heart gave out in the driveway of their home.

Maybe it was fear that had kept them together through the difficulties and challenges? She couldn't rightly pick it out from the mess of emotions that cycled in her mind and her heart.

Roger was bent forward, screaming. He felt it pinching his insides. He wanted to get it all out in a swift shout. The guilt that lived in him had set roots. And it had had enough time to drive deep into his being. In his cries, Roger felt the tangles gripping him, unwilling to give up their hold.

Danielle watched. Her husband sputtered and bellowed in his ragged voice. The thing in her stomach turned over, like a dead man lying face down in the dirt, moved to look up at the sky with an empty, sightless stare. It gave her pause. Her throat tightened. First James, now Roger was screaming.

The journey had taken so much out of all of them. It seemed the weary nights sleeping together in close quarters, the hot days of constant motion, and the endless road had taken its toll. So far as she could tell, the only one doing okay was herself. She grimaced at the sight of her husband. Now, on the verge of madness, dancing so near the edge of the precipice. She turned, looking back to the car with her sleeping children inside. She knew they still had further to go.

Roger stopped his screaming. His last cry sounded rough, like fabric being ripped down the middle. He shook, holding himself up by balancing on his knees. He wiped his forehead with his forearm, drawing the sweat from his brow. He panted like a drunk man who was still conscious when his stomach empties up his throat. The strange taste of digested food stabbed the senses. It's like a sudden shovel to the face that you can't make sense of. The mind reeling from the hard blow. It takes a moment to comprehend what just happened. Roger's legs shook, and his arms threatened to give out. His head hung down towards the ground. His shoulders arched as though the ridge in his spin was growing longer.

His breathing stuttered in his lungs, and he shivered in the morning air. Danielle made her way slowly towards him. He turned at the soft sound of her padding her way through the grass.

"This is my fault," said Roger. He gasped like a punctured balloon. Like it was his last words before dropping dead. Before the final nail was hammered into his coffin. Truthfully, he wondered how long he had wanted to confess to his wrongdoing. But there always seemed some reason to delay it a little longer, some excuse to hold onto the secret. Roger sat down in the grass. He put his face in both hands, smashing his features together as he gathered his long, unruly hair. He gathered everything in his hands. He pulled it all back and looked at his wife. Danielle stood a moment, then sat down beside Roger.

"Last night, I saw the horn glowing," he said. It was not the thing he had meant to tell her, but the truth still felt like it was too heavy to get out, at least without warming up to it first. "It might be done growing now." He was still shaken from his screaming session, and he had to clear his throat between words. Roger looked away from his wife several times before slowly turning back to face her. It was a lengthy process of Roger speaking and Danielle attentively listening.

"This is my fault," said Roger. He hung his head between his knees.

"We've had our difficulties," said Danielle. "I remember my mother telling my sister and me. It took a lot for her to stay with our father, but she said we're all just broken in the end. Some show it differently than others." She wiped at her nose, letting her mouth hang partly open. Roger nodded. He raised his shoulders and brought his chin closer to his collarbone. He looked as though he was trying to fold himself into a tiny square of paper. He started to pick at his hands.

"The night before this all started." Said Roger. He could sense his stomach muscles flexing as though in anticipation of a knife being stuck into his heart. He looked away from Danielle. His face contorted. He tried to turn back to deliver the final words, but he only managed to turn back to look at his hands in his lap. "I went out. I met this woman. I think we had sex. I can't remember it all." He started to increase his scratching at the back of his hands. The same childhood comfort brought him little satisfaction. He then had his hair back in his grasp and was pulling so hard that he could feel the pain in his nerves. The follicles being pulled out by the roots. He welcomed the pain. It was what he deserved. Roger ground his teeth, clenched his jaw, and breathed through his mouth. Something in him felt like it had become dislodged, but it still rattled inside him like a dead battery in a broken machine.

Danielle said nothing, but she also didn't look shocked by the delivery of information. She pinched at her chin, and her eyes were calm as she studied her husband's face.

"We're all broken," she said. "We're doing what we can to fix it." She gave him a frail smile. She took Roger's hand.

"We're in this together," she continued. "We can work on this. It hasn't been easy."

"No, it hasn't." They smiled at one another, and a brief laugh came to their eyes and cheeks. Roger leaned forward and kissed Danielle. "I promise I won't let anything come between us." She placed her hands on his long face and kissed him back. She briefly remarked about his whiskers scratching her face, but as they sat in that field, what Carter and James saw from the minivan windows was their parents sharing a passionate embrace.

Roger and Danielle could have remained in that state of loving bliss as the early morning mist slowly dissipated and the cool mid-morning sun warmed the grass and their backs. Birds whistled and chirped in the trees. They were both reluctant to turn back and see the minivan still waiting for them. It had become a hard jailer watching them in their brief recess. Now, they were being called back to their cell. Being forced to continue, to finish the journey.

There would be no true peace, no lasting rest so long as the brown minivan watched them. The parents stood, wiping their hands on their pants. The dewy grass stuck to their legs and their butts.

They thought secretly to themselves, what if we just ran away? What if we left the minivan here? Drop everything, get as far away from the trouble as we can? We could move somewhere where this thing would never find us. But it would be a searching eye, hungering for their sight. And though they thought this in secret, they both knew they had to stick to their parental duties. What would become of Carter if his horn was discovered? Every scientist in the world would be interested in cutting the boy open. They'd salivate at the chance to understand it. To try and make sense of what had inexplicably sprouted from the boy's forehead.

They somberly returned to the minivan. The heat of passion quickly dissipated and turned cold like an ember doused in water. Roger opened the door, and a painful lowing came from the back of the minivan.

11

Carter was groaning. He kicked the seat in front of him. He held his head.

"Fire. It burns! Too hot!" said Carter. His voice was muffled as though his throat was being squeezed. He groaned and wailed in the backseat.

"James, come up front," said Danielle. James moved from his seat next to Carter and went towards his mother. Roger was already out the door and going for the cold medicine they had picked up before. He took the box of medicine as well as the tape measurer from the hardware store back in the States. He intended to use it to measure growth of the horn, but now he wanted to use it to ensure the horn had stopped growing. He put the thought together in his mind that if the horn had truly stopped growing, it could hopefully explain what he had seen last night. The image of the glowing horn and fiery eyes staring at him put a lump in his throat. He swallowed hard. Carter went right on moaning, and Roger fumbled with the items.

He was breathing heavily. The voice that had hissed at him in the night, had it been a dream? He blinked and tried to focus on getting Carter the medicine.

Roger spilled some water from the bottle on his pants as he opened it. His hands shaking. He sat next to Carter, still moaning in pain. The horn stared at Roger. He blinked, and for a moment, he almost expected the horn to glow and blink back or to burst into fire. The hardened skin around the horn was stained red with Carter's continued scratching.

"How are you?" said Roger.

"Painful," said Carter. He winced.

"Did you sleep alright last night?" said Roger. He tried to mask the concern in his voice.

"I think so," said Carter after giving it some thought.

"Nothing strange? Dreams?"

"No, why?"

Roger gave his son the medicine, and Carter swallowed it with a gulp of water.

"Can I measure the horn?"

"Sure."

Roger held the tape measurer along the length of bone sticking out of the skin. He was suspicious he had not dreamed it glowing in the night. He couldn't bring himself to tell anyone other than Danielle what he saw. He didn't want to frighten his kids. The horn measured to a full six and a quarter inches in length. Roger felt dizzy, and his stomach rolled. He closed the tape measurer and reported his finding to Carter.

"How long is it going to keep growing?" asked Carter. His voice panged with concern, and his child's tone dropped. Carter lowered his eyes to look at his feet.

"Don't worry, this is almost over," said Roger. He moved and was just about to get out of the side door when Carter screamed. Roger, James, and Danielle jumped. The sound was like a glass vase knocked to the ground in a silent house. Carter's screaming took on a completely different voice than James's frustrated yells from the night before. Carter's screams were heart-rending, pain. His hands flew to his head. His teeth clicked as he clenched his jaw, baring his teeth. His eyes welled with tears and pain. Roger was back at his side. Carter breathed short breaths through his teeth. It sounded like a train picking up speed, charging along the tracks. Like a venomous snake hissing, dancing towards you.

Roger could see the tension in Carter's arms. He was desperately forcing both sides of his head together. Trying to keep it in one uniform shape. Like the seams had been ripped out, holding two sides of a cracking eggshell.

"We'll have to go to the hospital," shouted Roger.

Danielle turned in the driver's seat and looked over her shoulder at the father of her children. Carter trembled in the back seat. She opened her mouth as though she might try and offer a different solution, but everything was so loud and amplified in that small space. She turned the keys, and the van came to life. The old engine stuttered awake. They were moving once more.

James almost fell over at the speed that Danielle brought the van to. The tires squealed on the pavement. The engine roared. Roger held his son in the back seat, but he could do little to ease the pain.

"It's just a nightmare. Just a nightmare, you'll be okay," said Roger. Carter twisted and shook like he was shivering in a wind storm. There was so much force behind his movements. Roger's heart jumped against his chest. Outside the world started to rush by in greens, blues, and grays.

Everything was being shaken like beads in a kaleidoscope. Like tumbled rocks, breaking apart, ricocheting in every direction. Madness and chaos all around them. That was when, at that moment, Roger felt the presence of something even more terrible. He did not know whether his mind had finally had enough or if he had finally gone insane. But what Roger heard, like the faint drops of a first rain, was laughter.

A mocking voice seemed to ring in his ears, a witch's voice cackling from miles away at how successful her curse had been. The laughter roiled in his ears, now mixed with Carter's screaming, the engine roaring, and the beating of Roger's heart. All of which pounded and clawed at his senses. They were driving nails into him, and each one driven in brought a shot of pain. His nostrils flared, and his throat flexed.

From the front of the car, Danielle called his name. Ringing it like a bell. Roger, Roger, Roger. He had shut his eyes and was holding onto his son's shaking body. Doing everything in his power to keep the shattered pieces together. "It's just a nightmare, just a nightmare," Roger said repeatedly. He could never live with himself if Carter were to die. They had come all this way, keeping him safe, trying to protect his secret.

Both Roger and Danielle knew the pitying looks of strangers after a parent dies or is lost to madness. They had no choice. Now, they were going to have to bring Carter to the hospital. They were going to have to risk exposing the truth. Roger was seeing spots in the dark of his eyes. He listened to Danielle's plea-stricken voice. It was like crystal dropped from the top of a building. The single note it makes as it strikes the pavement. Fragile things, damaged beyond repair.

"What!?" shouted Roger. He opened his eyes. The world was still spinning, racing past in bright colors, a blur, and wash of sensation. Everything distorted like they were on a deranged, dark carnival ride.

"Are we really going to bring him to the hospital?" said Danielle.

"What choice?" He never finished his thought. Roger looked down and saw that the horn was glowing, and Carter's eyes had either rolled into his skull or clouded over with a white smoke. Carter's mouth was open. A bubbling froth-like foam was pushed out of his mouth like so much excreting waste and filth. It had the paste-like color of stomach bile mixed with snow. It was white and tainted a sickening yellow with a reddish hue. The boy's pulsations were still jerky. His head appeared much too heavy for his neck. Each time he pulsed from deep within, Carter's head launched forward like a striking axe.

Danielle struggled to keep her eyes on the road. Her gaze lingered in the rearview mirror. And she fought the urge to swing around in her seat and see the horrific scene of her child in pain. Her stomach flexed, and she felt each outburst like a knife cutting through her. Like a bullet passing through the lungs, tearing out the vocal cords. A knife that stuck under her ribs and slipped between her bones. It twisted in her, driving and seeking her heart.

She kept her hands clenched on the wheel. Her arms threatened to give out, but the rest of her was solid as stone. Her foot increased the speed.

The needle on the speedometer climbed. The engine was hot, but Danielle did not ease the tension in her body. The spike of adrenaline in her now was the kind that could let her lift a tractor-trailer on her own to save her children. They were fortunate to be racing in such a remote part of the world. There was such little traffic that they came across that Danielle could easily maneuver the car to the left before swinging it back into the driving lane. A sudden shriek of sirens split the air.

However, the sound was insignificant to both Danielle and Roger. Roger still heard only the bubbling laughter that splintered in his ears. Danielle heard only the crying outbursts of her oldest son. They were both deaf to any other stimulus.

Red and blue lights flashed behind them. Danielle did not stop. She did not slow in the slightest. The minivan shook like the bolts were being unscrewed, as though at any moment, the six-hundred-dollar monstrosity would fall apart. At any moment, the engine would stall, and they would be stuck on the road, with their son frothing at the mouth. Eyes rolled back into his head. The screams, the sirens, the blood-curdling terror rising in their chests. Then everything stopped. The world spun so fast that time and space became a still-frame picture. Movement and motion, caught in a sudden freeze frame.

The road had abruptly expanded like a throat, leading to an enlarged gullet. Like a snake suddenly opening its jaws to swallow its prey whole. What was two lanes flooded like blood spilled across a tile floor. Six lanes of traffic ran north-south. They had been driving west at breakneck speeds. Police sirens still in hot pursuit. Danielle had not been able to manage the turn that was meant to be taken at 40 KPH. She had clipped the railing and swung the car on two wheels to avoid the ditch in the median between traffic and road.

The van spun around, launched into the air, rolled, jumped, and ground along the ground. Sparks shot in on them. Shards of glass glittered like fire sparklers. They were rag dolls being shaken in a burlap bag. Roger shielded his eyes, but glass shot in and cut across his forearms. He felt the bite of glass at his hands, a finger was severed. The van was still moving like a train that had run out of track. Wheels that had gone bare, metal spinning against metal. The grating noise rang out all around like a bell being tolled from a high clock tower in a dark town, with a fiery, red-blood moon rising over a demonic church. Still, the laughter persisted. It boiled in Roger's ears. It cried out in his mind, and it raked its long nails across his senses.

Then there was silence.

12

Roger's breath burned in his lungs. He blinked in the carnage.
They were upside down. James lay on the roof of the car. His
head was tucked into his arm. Roger could not tell if he was
breathing. Nothing seemed to be moving. His throat was
closing, and the world faded like everything was taking a long
blink. A slow closing of the eye, ready for an eternal sleep.
Someone stood outside. The crunch of boots on glass made
Roger turn his head. Carter was next to Roger. He looked with
a trembling fist welling in his throat. Carter was also not

moving. He was on his back. Staring up with those milk-white eyes.

Slowly, as though moving through a dream, Roger unclipped himself from his seat belt. He dropped to the ceiling. There was a burning sensation in his left hand. Like a piece of it had been dipped in gasoline and lit. It was a pain that felt branded into him. A deep wound that would forever leave its mark. The pink skin never able to fully heal. He would always bear this sign. It would be evidence of the struggle of the trip they had taken. Something to be marveled at in years to come.

Roger was on his belly. The familiar smell of sweat, stale air, and heat still lingered. But now it mixed with new pungent odors, salt, and the dust of stones, the black tar heat that rises from roads baked in sunlight. Ancient things crushed under tires. Their guts dragged and dispersed across the continents like handfuls of ash. There was a rattling in Roger's chest. Some muscle he had never known he was capable of flexing twitched. Or maybe his upper ribs had shifted in the crash. He could not make out the sensation properly.

"Danielle?" said Roger. "James? Carter?" There was no response from the other three. His voice shook as he called out again. "Danielle? Carter? James?" He crawled to James. He hadn't moved since Roger had started to move about. "James?

Danielle? Carter?" His voice spiked with fear. And still, there was no response. The black boots outside kicked at clusters of broken glass. A face peered in from the broken window.

"Don't move. We'll get you out of there," said the man with the black boots. Roger held James to his chest. His insides burned. They were being devoured in a strong, hot acid that burrowed through him. It left nothing behind. Roger held James. He hugged him tightly, and he turned his face towards him. He looked at the adolescent child face of his youngest son. He loved them. He loved James, Carter, and Danielle. He pressed his face into James's. Tears streaked down his face. His body trembled and shook.

His breathing clipped through trembling lips. He was a toothless man muttering to himself. An image of Roger flickered in his addled brain. For a brief instant, he saw himself years in the future. All long, gray hair matted and tangled like thick jungle vines. He would be sightless, toothless, and wandering the wastes of the world. This would be his punishment.

Then there were many hands. Eyes from strangers looked in on the family. They reached in, extended with delate care not to aggravate any more damage. Trying to pick fragments of pottery off the floor of an archeological find. The dirt and dust needing to be brushed away with feather dusters. So it was how Roger and the rest of his family were removed from the overturned minivan.

Roger closed his eyes and surrendered to the darkness that flooded his mind. He sensed it close in on him like a tidal wave crashing with thunder and fury. He tried to force his mind to focus on breathing. His lungs felt tired like a balloon rapidly filled and deflated several times. Like a belly that has over-expanded. A tumor that has suddenly disappeared in the middle of the night or doubled in size.

There was so much empty space in him. He shivered. He was nothing more than a husk, a hollowed-out tree stump. He was a gaping hole. There was the feeling of motion. The hands that had reached in and pulled him delicately from the tomb of the brown minivan had lifted him. He had felt the warm sun on his skin for a brief number of steps. It had flooded his closed eyes, trying to penetrate the darkness. It had felt pleasant. The touch of sunlight, like a caressing hand brushing his face, calling him towards heaven.

They laid him onto a board, moving him like an extracted sarcophagus. They had prepared them all for transport. He had been lifted once more, raised, and set in the back of a metal box. His mind wavered, teetering on the edge of consciousness like a child balancing over a slender wood bridge. He reached out, touching the edge with his mind. Reaching his feet to hang over the edge of the drop-off.

There was pressure on his hand. Without opening his eyes, Roger could sense someone sitting next to him, touching him like a slab of meat ready for inspection. He was a loaf of bread being pinched and prodded. A sharp pressure pinched down on his hand. He flinched away. Something had bitten him. Whatever was seated next to him persisted. It reached out, drawing his hand back towards it.

Roger again focused his attention on the act of breathing. It was something he had never had to devote much thought to before. Something you were born knowing, but now the act took much of his mental concentration to ensure the draw and release of air circulating through his body.

The pinch of pressure and bite of pain was back at his hand. He wondered how deep the teeth might be reaching. Were they striking bone? Gnawing away like a dog on a cow's femur. Chewing the bones to splinters.

The image of a blood moon rising over a dark steeple came to his mind. He now stood in the courtyard, staring at that red moon. It looked to be dripping, falling down upon the dark, silent town. The red light was everywhere, and still, nothing but shadows stood out from the night. In Roger's mind, he stood looking up at the church steeple. He heard the tolling bell ring in his mind.

Faint, so faint, he had to guess at words. Something was speaking his name. But it was like he was listening from underwater. A jumbled, warble of inaudible syllables. Standing in the doorway of this imagined church, bathed in blood red moonlight, was the monster that had looked at Roger. He felt hands on his chest. The person that had sat beside him and tended to his lost finger was now restraining him.

Roger twisted and convulsed on the board. He pulled and fought against the straps that held him in place. His forehead had been strapped down, and he fervently fought against it. He squirmed and wriggled like a worm being burned under a magnifying glass. The glowing horn stared at him from the church steps. He was helpless to its stare.

He opened his eyes and mouth. He drew short, ragged breaths that rattled in his throat. Even with his eyes open, he felt the burning stare of the horned monster. He blinked, trying to let his eyes adjust to the light in the ambulance. But his eyes were slow to focus. Every inch of him was screaming with fatigue. The back of his skull was starting to feel bruised, as though a thumbprint had been roughly pressed against the spot where his head touched the board. He clenched his teeth, still fighting against the straps, still fighting against the burning stare. He was like a mental patient rolling around on the floor; arms bound to his chest by the straightjacket.

The horn blinked, wreathed in fire. He struggled harder, but the man sitting beside him held the straps down. Thunder and lightning was striking in Roger's mind. Were they dead? Could they all be dead?

His eyes met the eyes of the EMT. He saw now, as her image came into focus, that she was not a man. A strong, stern-faced woman with blonde hair pulled back. Her face looked weathered by horror. It had the mark of brutality witnessed again and again.

"Can you tell me?" said Roger. The sound of his voice was detached from his own thoughts. His tongue ground like ancient gears coated with rust. Forcefully pressing against the wearing of time. Countless days abandoned to the elements. To the onslaught of wind, snow, and rain. He was speaking like a man who had just woken after a year. Or a hundred years lost to dreaming. He was captured in time. He helplessly looked at the face of the woman beside him. Tears welled in his eyes. His vision blurred. The stare was on him again.

His eyes grew like he was staring into the headlight of a train moving so fast that he wouldn't feel a thing as his bones broke all at once. His breathing was shallow, like his lungs were leaking air. Why couldn't the witch – why couldn't she have cursed him with the horn? Why did she have to make him suffer this way? His heart pounded in his chest like war drums. Marching like armies ready to kill. His hands were one of the few parts of him that he had full range of. He balled his fingers into fists until they both shook at his sides. He breathed through clenched teeth. Anger, fire, and hatred burned in his mind.

"Are they alive?" asked Roger. Roger's strength left him. He closed his eyes, listening to the sound of his own breathing. Waiting for the woman to respond. The sound of his heart kicking in his chest. It was like a switch had been pulled, and his body was shutting down. His fists unclenched and lay against the board. He no longer struggled against the straps. He lay in that darkness, letting it envelop him with its embrace. He drank it in with each breath. Like smoke from a wood fire, it filtered in through his body. And he could feel it traveling along his arms, filling the chambers of his head and his chest. He sensed it traveling the channels of his veins, making its way along each extremity like he was a gallery of paintings.

Roger waited and listened. There was no response. The woman said nothing, and Roger heard nothing. His mind surrendered and welcomed the darkness, and Roger slept briefly, fitfully. He was back in that dark town with the crimson moon tinting the world in blood and shadow. The red glow chilling the world in an everlasting night. A tide that would never lower. A night that would never fade.

In his sleeping, Roger walked the streets. Every road and street appeared abandoned. Nothing but bleak, empty darkness lived here. Then Roger turned his face towards the swollen moon. He thought he had caught the hint of a shadow pass across the face. He blinked, staring at the blazing moon.

A low sound like whispers spoken at a distance, just on the edge of hearing, filtered down from overhead. Building like a cauldron slowly roiling. Roger braced himself. His whole body tensed, prepared for impact. He guessed at what passed across the glow of the moon. It flew on a broomstick. The laughter turned his gut. Now, it was boiling over. The anger returned to him. Even in his dreams, he could feel his muscles tightening. Flexing like a tiger stalking its prey. Silently pawing the jungle ground, creeping ever closer to the act of killing. The idea burned in him like a jewel. Something stirred to life. A desire that he had managed to keep at bay.

His thoughts drifted to the sleeping man. How his body had quivered with satisfaction in the act of killing. He was now hungry for more.

13

A bright light shone on Roger. Clean, untainted light covered him. Gradually, he heard the roll of air through his body and the hum of machinery. Footsteps on a hard floor. His hand itched. The one that had been chewed at when he was lying in the ambulance. His body shook as he tried to move. Everything was sore. His neck, his back, and even his eyes felt sore. The insides of his eyelids were also itchy, but he didn't have the strength to rub them.

A chill lay over him like a thin layer of ice. He feared if he opened his eyes, he would see his body replaced by metal and wires. It was a feeling that his skin had been stripped away and replaced by a metallic alloy.

He twisted in his bed, the knots in his muscles strained as he reached for his hand. Of course, the finger that he reached for was not there. It only existed at this point in his mind. A phantom pain like a bad memory lingered. He wondered if he thought back if he could pinpoint the exact moment when his finger was separated from the rest of his body. He wondered if it might be somewhere, like a lit cigarette on the minivan's floor.

He winced, jumping back from probing his mind. The minivan felt like a live wire. He avoided the thought. He let out a breath and opened his eyes. White walls jumped at him from all sides. The light overhead brought a hot fever to his brow. He blinked and gaped at the ceiling.

He frowned, still looking up, still disoriented, grasping desperately at what had happened. He lay there, lost in thought. The pieces felt disjointed, like the puzzle kept changing no matter what he did. The moment he put together a string of thoughts, something would change, and it would be all wrong.

Slowly, he started to move a little more. His body had not been replaced with gears or mechanisms of any kind, but his hand had been wrapped and bandaged. His stiff body protested the movement. Roger clicked his teeth when the pain lanced through him like a bullet. He actively worked against the will of his body. Forcing the stiff joints to bend and move despite their reluctance.

His eyes focused better, and the harsh light felt less intrusive. He reshaped his own form in his mind. He had pulled his own body from a shallow grave. He turned his head and watched a screen display his vital signs. The machine hummed away to itself, pulsing and beeping, measuring his heartbeat. Roger could not keep the thoughts at bay for very long, and misery looked in on him like a killer with empty, sightless eyes. He weakly flexed his hands. He sat up in bed, pulling the wires out of him.

The machine flat-lined making a terrible pitch. He swung his feet over the side of his bed. He tried to stand, but his head spun viciously. He had to cling to the bedside to keep from falling to the floor. His legs were not able to hold his weight. He slid down, still holding to the bedside, towards the ground. He just managed to drape himself on the edge of the bed. His nose hovering just above the plastic mattress. It had a sickly smell to it, like defecation, like bodily fluids, like blood, and death.

After a moment, he managed to get his legs properly under him again, all the while breathing in the horrible scent of death masked only slightly by disinfectant. His head spun more fervently with each inhale. It was a toxin seeping into his brain, clouding his senses with its noxious green cloud. It choked him like smog over a city.

His legs trembled, and it took all the strength he could muster to push himself away from the bed and stand upright. His legs threatened to buckle. He locked his knees and walked bow-legged towards the door. Roger teetered like a drunk man; his arms extended as though he was balancing on a tightrope.

He paused there, his hand on the door handle. The idea of what lay beyond the door was like a body in the moonlight. He half turned towards the bed. He looked away from the cold, hard truth that was waiting for him. Crouched in the darkness just beyond the room. His stomach bubbled, and he winced from the lance of pain in his chest. He turned the handle. He had to know. He would have to face the truth sooner or later. He pulled the door open and staggered out into a fluorescent-lit hallway.

More clean, white walls reflected back at him. A nurse passed by, stopping in her quick pace. She turned to look at Roger. He was standing with his legs awkwardly bent as though his femurs had snapped and healed at odd angles.

"Are you alright?" said the nurse. Roger shifted his weight from side to side. His head felt swollen. He let his chin drop to his chest. The muscles in his neck were too weak to lift the massive weight of his head. He stood there unsure, simply trying to keep himself upright.

The nurse took Roger by the elbow.

"Let's get you back in your room," she said. He wanted to say something, but his words stuck in his throat. His mouth could not open fully, and his tongue was reluctant to move. It clumsily tried to make sounds, but all Roger could do was mumble to himself. The nurse led Roger back into his room and sat him back in his bed. He had made no progress, but he caught how the nurse looked at him as she studied the clipboard at the end of his bed. She didn't have to say anything. Roger knew they were all dead. He put his head in his hands and cried.

14

Roger bleated like a cow cut down the side. Blood pounding out of the wound with each pulse of an enlarged heart. The pain like a line of fire being dragged across the body by a long, pointed forefinger. He grabbed at his hair and pulled until it hurt. He deserved more pain. He scratched his hands. The hope he had so desperately clung to, that they would all be alright, broke like fine China glass. The damage so extensive, it could never be set right. He bit his tongue hard. He wanted to cry. He wanted to feel the misery racking its cold fingers through him.

He wanted it to pile stones in his stomach. He shook there on the bed. His hands clenched as though each held a blood-stained knife. As though he had been the one to kill them all.

As though in a fit of madness, he barricaded the front door and slowly crept into each of their rooms. In the dark of the night, with the moonlight on their sleeping faces, he had been the one to kill them. Silently going from room to room until all that remained were still bodies.

But it had not been a slow death. It had been a quick, painless one. The minivan had become the tomb and the killer. He thought back in his mind; this time, he was certain he could pinpoint the exact moment when Danielle, James, and Carter screamed for the last time. Just before the glass flew in on them. Just before their heads struck metal, or pavement. The hot spray of sparks melting them like plastic toys.

He cried until he tasted blood rising on the back of his tongue. He mashed his face and his eyes with his hands. Nothing would help. Nothing could bring them back. Roger heaved, blinking with sandy, raw, red eyes. His mouth quivered as though he was still mumbling to himself. The nurse said nothing but stood at the foot of the bed, head tilted to the clipboard. Her eyes glanced with that pitying look.

"Just tell me! Please tell me!" Said Roger. He looked at the nurse like she had pulled him from a river. Like she had saved him. He trembled like a relapsing druggie, Just trying to get his next fix so that he could stop the shakes for a moment. "Please, tell me, is my family dead?" he swallowed.

"You were all in quite the car crash," said the nurse. "It's amazing you survived."

"I wasn't supposed to!" he cried out. "I should be dead!"

Roger let his head fall limp. His outburst left him with a tremor. He could feel his heartbeat ticking away in his throat. Then silence drifted into the room. It reached in, slipping through the crack under the door. It entered from the window. She lay her body across the floor and began to expand, filling the room with her grim, bitter presence.

He could feel the silence touch him. She wrapped her arms around his neck, leaning forward and breathing her cold breath into his mouth. She filled him with stuffing and ragweed. It tasted bitter. Roger and the nurse exchanged occasional glances as the silence held them captive.

"The bodies?" asked Roger after some time passed. Though, he would have believed the world frozen in time. That all the clocks had reached their final conclusion. There were no more seconds, minutes, or hours to be counted. He blinked, hands on his thighs, kept prisoner to the silence that had placed icy river stones in his belly. He pressed his tongue against the roof of his mouth. His breathing slowed, and Roger managed to unclench his jaw. He breathed in through his mouth, but it no longer sounded like a snake hiss. He wiped at his face. "Can I see them?"

"Let me check your vitals first," she said. She felt his pulse, and had him track her finger with his eyes. Roger did everything she asked and allowed her to pinch and prod him. "Any pain?"

"Sore, but I'll pull through." He gave a weak look of disinterest. He knew he was forever going to be the one left behind. The one burdened with the memories of the guilt, the good, and the bad times. At least before, they all shouldered the secrets of what they had done. Of who they had become together. Now, he was left to pick up the pieces.

The nurse brought him a wheelchair and helped him into it.

"Are you sure you want to see them now?"

"Yes."

Roger was wheeled out of the room and brought along a hallway. On both sides were many rooms. Sometimes, the doors were open. They offered brief glimpses into the sick and dying. The word lucky that the nurse had used stuck at him like the least likely word to describe the whole situation. Anyone who ended up in a hospital was unlucky. There was little to no luck to ever be found in hospitals, he thought. Roger started to think of all the things that would be, in fact, lucky.

If they had never had to come on this trip in the first place. If Carter had never complained about a headache. If his head had never split open. If they were all still alive. If he had never had his own secret. If he had never drank Lucile's wine. If he had never been involved with her in the first place. He turned the blame over and over in his mind until the thought started to glow with a living fire. He knew he was getting dangerously close to remembering the heat of the stare of that monster with the glowing horn. Was that what Carter was being turned into?

Maybe they had been lucky?

The guilt stirred in him, boiling with heat. Hot coals were dropped in one by one, and each glowing ember raised the temperature a little more than before. Roger held his head in his hands as his nurse wheeled him down to the morgue. The pungent smell of decay and refrigeration coolant wafted like a mist as they made their way down the last tunnel.

It had the feeling of being swallowed, moving slowly towards a brightly lit room at the end of a dark passageway. The temperature dropped noticeably as they made their way deeper into the hospital's underground. The nurses' footsteps clicked on the cement floor. Then they were in the crypt.

A man with a graying goatee met them by the entrance. His hair formed a horseshoe-like wreath around his bald scalp. Roger blinked. The sight was like being drowned. Having his head forcibly jammed under the ice of a frozen lake. Eyes peeled open and forced to stare at the haunted, ghostly faces underneath the surface. He was staring death in the face. He choked a moment, coughing and sputtering at the fragrance of bodies decomposing. It reminded him of how it might feel to be buried alive. The smell of earth above. Worms crawling through the walls.

You scream, but all that fills your mouth is dirt and darkness. No one hears your cry. But there was light. A room with chrome doorways that lead to more rooms. Side rooms lined with shelves, metal tables, scales, and wide-angle cameras. The dead would be processed through here like the gates of Saint Peter. Their weathered faces were caught on film.

Roger wavered in the doorway. He blinked. His mind worked furiously at the thought that any of this could happen in a modern world. How many rooms were there like this in the country? In the world? How many refrigerated rooms kept bodies cold like unfinished glasses of milk?

And how many of them had already decomposed sleeping men? He felt the pinch in his stomach like fire on the other side of a wall. Its presence rose in him. He looked down the side rooms as far as he could see. He pressed his tongue against his teeth, but the feeling remained. The feeling that he was being watched. That in the corner of one of these dark spaces was a monster crouched on all fours, silently waiting for its chance to jump out and gobble him up.

"They're this way," said the man, motioning for Roger and the nurse to follow him. The nurse wheeled Roger behind the attendant. The three entered through a doorway, and there on a set of metal tables were Danielle, James, and Carter. They looked like manikins waiting to be properly stood up. Their bodies were still, with no hint of life to be found.

Roger stared without words. There were no thoughts in his mind. He looked at his dead family like an empty vessel. He was so cold that he expected to see his breath fog in front of his eyes. His tongue went slack in his mouth, and the only thing

Roger could do was look. He leaned forward in his wheelchair, lacing his fingers together.

"Why?" Said Roger. "Why! Why! Why! Why! Why!" He struck his forehead with the bridge of his hands. Like a hammer trying to pound a nail, Roger tried to beat an answer into his skull. He fought back the tears, but just barely. His mouth tasted metallic, like his lip was bleeding. Like he tasted blood. He felt the stare of guilt. He knew the dreaded monster was in the room with them. He could turn and look upon the glowing horn.

Carter lay on a table, and the dreadful horn was still sticking out like an embedded shard of rock. It was no longer the color of fresh bone. With its host dead, the horn had blackened and turned the color of a dead fingernail. It looked like a chunk of metal from the car wreck had shot into the boy's brain. Killing him instantly. But Roger knew the truth. He knew in his heart who had been the one to kill them.

"I did this," said Roger. "I killed them! I killed them all." Roger stood from his wheelchair. He pointed to the bodies on the tables, the ones of his family. Then he pointed to the shelves. He pointed to the bodies already wrapped in bags with tags hanging from their toes. "I killed each and every one of them."

"This can be hard on people," said the nurse. She was strong but caring. "I'll take you back to your room." Roger didn't sit down. He remained standing, looking around at the lifeless bodies. His eyes fell on the black horn. The curse that was meant for him. He moved towards the table where Carter lay in his eternal sleep. Had Lucille meant everything to go like this? Had her curse been strong enough to kill his entire family and leave him unscathed? He hated Lucille. He hated that he had fallen into it. He wished he'd just gone to bed that night. It felt so long ago, but that night would forever haunt Roger. His fingers curled as though he was holding a knife. The thought brought a fire to him.

He reached out a hand, unclenching his fingers, and touched the black bone in his son's forehead. It was hard and pointed as slate. Roger closed his eyes and touched the face of his oldest son. He ran his fingers over the grotesque horn. His breath shuttered through him. Then he bent down and kissed Carter for the last time on the side of his cheek. He touched the hard carapace that formed and the marks left from Carter's scratching. He turned away and went to James. His youngest son was unchanged from when Roger had held him to his chest in the wreckage of the minivan. The trip had been doomed from the start. His shoulders raised as Roger stood by his son. He touched James's face, still breathing soft and low. Struggling to keep the tears from flooding his eyes. He had done so much crying. His lungs were fatigued, and his eyes felt blistered by hot sun and sand.

Then he shuffled to the table where his wife lay. Roger could not keep back the tears. His voice broke.

"We're all just broken," he said. He pressed his forehead against the forehead of his wife and cried. When he regained his breath, he collapsed back into the wheelchair. He sniffed and wiped at his face even though it hurt.

"We'll need some more time before we're ready to move forward with any of them," said the nurse. She spun Roger around and wheeled him back to his room. She put him back into his bed. Roger's body was so wracked from his emotions that every part of him shook. Even lying in bed took a large amount of effort. His arms wouldn't stay still at his sides, and Roger looked up at the ceiling until he surrendered to sleep again.

He preferred sleeping to being awake. It was less painful. He could dream that he had done everything right. He could dream that he had never come across that witch. His sleep soon became plagued with dark nightmares of killing and revenge. He no longer feared the monster with its glowing horn. He was the monster, and he was something to be feared.

Over the next week, Roger felt his strength return. He could soon walk without an aide, and his nurse visits became merely check-ins. He met with a psychiatrist to help with the emotions of coping with the loss of his family. Roger felt he was making good strides to recover from the accident, but there was a gnawing feeling in his heart. Something that wouldn't go away.

When night settled, he would look out into the dark sky. He would look up to the moon and remember the blood moon with the town made of shadows. The church with its pointed steeple. And he would remember the shadow that Lucille cast as she flew across that moon. Each night, he looked with dread at the pale, round orb. Each night he expected to see some shadow fly across its face. He tried not to look at the moon. He tried to push it from his mind, but the feeling lingered.

Towards the end of the week, Roger made his way back to the morgue alone. His stomach still twisted as he neared the smell of decay and refrigeration coolant. He knew he would have to make arrangements for a burial. He would have to sign off on the bodies being moved. He met with the man with the silver goatee. He asked if something could be done about the piece sticking out of his son's forehead. The man told him it was not something they could do here, but once the bodies were shipped to a funeral home, they would easily be able to remove it.

Another week later, Roger and the bodies of his family were ready to leave. Roger had the horn removed from Carter's head. The growth was cut out and tossed away, but Roger retrieved it. For hours, he held the strange object in his hands. He turned it over, looking at it from every possible angle. He felt its weight in his hand. He almost had to laugh at how minute the horn felt in his hands. How insignificant it was now that it had been pulled from Carter's head.

That night, Roger stared at the moon. He watched it rise. Not once did he turn away from its glow. He thought about what he had to do. He felt the desire take hold of him. It was now a part of his being. He knew he would never be able to have a moment's peace until he took the cursed horn and drove it deep into the witch's heart.

END

www.ingramcontent.com/pod-product-compliance
Lightning Source LLC
Chambersburg PA
CBHW062215150726
47991CB00006B/2288